I0526646

# THE PIANO PLAYER

*A Jacob Schreiber Mystery*

By

# Guy Beaulieu

W & B Publishers
USA

W & B Publishers

For information:
W & B Publishers
Post Office Box 193
Colfax, NC 27235
www.a-argusbooks.com

ISBN: 978-0-6159484-5-4
ISBN:  0-6159484-5-6

Book Cover designed by Dubya

Printed in the United States of America

# DEDICATION

As always, to my wife Inge

And, to the memory of Donald K. Ryle, a friend

ACKNOWLEDGEMENTS:

The author wishes to thank:

Gwen MacPherson for her professional proof-reading.

DAVID BELL for his friendship and advice.

My son John for his technical guidance.

## CHAPTER ONE

Disturbingly for Lieutenant Bill Jones finding dead bodies on the streets of L.A. was considered part of his job description. The problem in most cases was how the person had died. The majority of the time it was a violent death. January of this year was no better than the same month the year before. In the early hours of January 4 in the back alley of The Red Dahlia—a favorite hangout for tango lovers in West Los Angeles—it happened again. Carl Murdoch's body had been found, hands tied behind his back and mouth gagged. Three bullet holes were visible to the eye. One through the throat, one through the heart and a third one in the private parts. Which one was fired first would only be a guess. One thing was certain, they were all fired at close range. Murdoch was a musician who sometimes filled in for the piano player at the Red Dahlia so the trio of bass, sax and piano could stay intact. No one ever noticed the difference as Carl played in the same manner as the regular trio member did. From the information he could muster up, Lieutenant Jones did not have much to go on. The victim was known to the patrons of the bar as a quiet, friendly man in his fifties who never said a bad word about anyone. The condition the body was found in told a different story. No one had heard anything. No noise, no gunshots and not even an argument. Now why would a man who appeared to be liked by everyone and known for his mild outgoing nature be murdered in a gangland style fashion? Jones would have to search the man's background, and possibly, the FBI prints files for clues.

It was a frisky morning, perfect for taking a walk. Exactly what Private Investigator Jacob Schreiber had decided to do instead of driving to the office. On his twenty-minute journey down Hollywood Boulevard, he always encountered an array of personalities. Yes, plethora of personalities: drunks, drug addicts, prostitutes and people sleeping on the sidewalk who either could not get home or did not have a home. Before entering his office building he went to the coffee shop for his morning fix of dark roast and doughnuts, picked up a morning paper and ran up the stairs to his second floor office. The door was unlocked which meant his secretary was at her desk.

"Good morning, Anne. How was the theater play last night?" Jacob asked.

Anne answered, "Not bad, my husband stayed awake for a change. You had a couple of telephone calls so far this morning. One is from Lieutenant Jones and the second from a Mrs. Claudette Bailey of Pacific Palisades. She would like to talk to you before noon today. Anything new on the wedding arrangements?"

"We are planning for March if all goes well. It's unfortunate Lorraine's sister got in a bad car accident, otherwise last Thanksgiving would have been the day. With no other family around and the two sisters being so close, it was better that we delayed the arrangements. Colette is going back to practicing law next week. I am glad that ordeal is over. Could you get this Mrs. Bailey on the telephone?" the gumshoe asked his secretary.

"Good morning Mrs. Bailey this is Jacob Schreiber, how can I be of help to you?" he asked.

Mrs. Bailey said, "You were recommended to me by a good friend who is a bank president up your way. I live in the Palisades on a four-acre estate and have five servants working for me on a regular basis. Three days ago some of my antique and valuable jewelry disappeared and I would like you to investigate the situation. Could you come by this afternoon? We can settle your fee then, if you decide to take on my case. I really wish you would since I know about your integrity," concluded a worried woman.

Jacob answered, "Would 2 o'clock be suitable for you Mrs. Bailey? Good, I'll see you this afternoon."

Next, he called his friend Lieutenant Bill Jones of the LAPD homicide division.

"Jacob here, Lieutenant, I'm returning your call. Anything urgent you wanted to talk about?" the private eye asked.

The homicide detective said, "It's nice to hear from you this early. I know you are an early bird. Last year if you recall your name kept surfacing all over the place. Usually where dead men were found. I was very happy to see the trend come to a stop. Well, guess what, my friend, your business card was found again in the pockets of a dead musician in the wee hours of the morning. I have but one question for you, are you a psychic? Do you go around giving your business card to people you know will be murdered? Okay. Okay. In a very sad situation I am trying to be funny, and obviously by the dead sound on the telephone line, not very successful at it, either," concluded the LAPD Lieutenant.

Jacob said, "Well, Lieutenant, if only I could see that clearly into the future, we could avoid all the hard work we are faced with day in, day out. Is it someone I know personally, a former client maybe?"

"Does the name Carl Murdoch ring a bell with you, Jacob?"

"Carl Murdoch, Carl Murdoch, I've heard that name before but I can't place him right now. Did you say he was a musician? What instrument did he play? Was he in a band or just a solo guy?" The private eye asked.

"I don't have answers to all of your questions, Jacob, but can tell you he was a piano player. Most of his playing time was done at the Red Dahlia in West Los Angeles. They have a regular trio that plays there four nights a week. At times, he stood in for the regular piano player. His body was found in a back alley behind the building where the bar is located. He had been gagged and shot three times. In his pocket was one of your business cards. That's why I thought you may have known the guy," the detective concluded.

"As I said, Lieutenant, the name is familiar, but I can't place a face with it yet. It may be that I saw a poster sometime ago with his name on it. I suppose you want me to come to the morgue and possibly identify the body? OK, I'll do that on my way to see a client in the Palisades, say around one o'clock? If not, it will have to be tomorrow," said the private eye.

The Lieutenant answered, "One o'clock is fine; see you then, Jacob."

When Anne walked into his office bringing correspondence for him to review, he said to her, "Can you believe this, the LAPD finds a murdered man and guess what?"

Anne quickly said, "He had your business card in his pocket?"

They looked at each other in disbelief.

Jacob said, "Does the name Carl Murdoch ring a bell with you Anne?"

"We had a client by the name of Murdoch when I first started working with you, but I don't recall the name Carl," Anne said. "Let me get the file and we'll see." She went to the filing cabinet and returned with a smile on her face. "Here it is boss, William Peter Murdoch. You helped him find some missing recording equipment and original music sheets. In fact, it's written in here that instead of cash payment you took four albums that he had produced. One of them was about the big band style music and featured a piano player by the name of...Carl Murdoch. It also says in here they were brothers." Anne handed the file to her boss.

"Wow," Jacob said, "that was a long time ago. I recall doing the job for that kind of payment because Peter Murdoch had been in the Navy during the war. He was a darn good musician himself and built a recording studio to help up-and-coming young performers. Peter Murdoch was in his mid-thirties or early forties and Carl, I recall now, was the older brother of four. Yeah, I do have his album at home and he was a fantastic performer. I also remember Peter telling me he kept Carl around the recording studio to help with the younger musicians. Here, I have a telephone number where to reach Peter."

Jacob dialed the number and a woman answered. There was no one there by the name of Peter. She had this number for over a year now. He put the telephone down and looked through the file for the address of the recording studio. Here it was, underlined; on Santa Monica Boulevard five blocks from the ocean.

"After I'm done with Mrs. Bailey I'm going to drive by Peter's old recording studios. I cannot believe he closed it all down. It looked like a thriving business at the time. Funny how things go, Anne. I told Jones that the name Murdoch rang a bell with me but could not remember. I wonder if Peter is still around. Recording studios are almost like restaurants. They pop up all over the place and disappear just as fast."

Anne rushed back to her desk to answer the telephone.

"Jacob, it's for you; a George Murdoch is on the line," Anne said.

"Jacob Schreiber here. Yes, Mr. Murdoch, I remember your brother Peter but I believe we have not met before. What can I do for you?" he paused, then said in response to the caller, "I'm very sorry about that. I heard from the LAPD about your brother Carl. I should be back in my office by 4 p.m. today. Good, I'll see you then, Mr. Murdoch."

So one of the brothers wanted to have a talk with Jacob because he did not believe the police would work too hard trying to find out who murdered his brother Carl. Brother George had said he would fill in the details in the office later today.

"Anne, better open a new file with the name Murdoch on it. I have a feeling we are—at least I am—going to be pretty busy. Whatever you have in the one file not related to the original case, transfer to the new one."

Jacob just let his mind freely wander about the Murdoch family. He could not remember anything that would cause Carl to be murdered the way he was. Jacob placed his .45 back into a shoulder holster, got his jacket and told his secretary he was on his way to lunch with a friend, the morgue and then the Pacific Palisades to meet his new client.

*Claudette Bailey,* he thought, *I remember looking at an old silent film where the movie star was a Claudette Bailey. I wonder if it's the same person. This is not an unusual name but out here in Hollywood, one never knows what comes with a name.*

After eating lunch with an old school friend he had not seen in some time, he drove to downtown LA to the morgue where Lieutenant Bill Jones was waiting for him.

"I read in the paper, Jacob, that you refused the presidency of the Little League," said the detective. "Not up to it, or too busy to make a full commitment? Which is it, my friend?"

Jacob answered, "I would not be able to give it my full attention. I prefer staying on the coaching side of things. This way I can interact much more with a small group of kids and give them the attention they need. Since we talked this morning, my memory came back. I had a client by the name of Peter Murdoch who had three brothers one of which was Carl the piano player. For the work I did with this Peter Murdoch, I took in payment three albums he had recorded in his Santa Monica studio. One of the albums was about the big band music played during the war and it featured Carl Murdoch at the piano. Strange how small the world can get at times, don't you think, Lieutenant?"

"Tell me about it, we do live in strange times. Let's go to the frozen gallery here and see if you recognize this body," Jones said.

After staring at the body for what seemed to be a long time, Jacob said, "Did you notice the tattoos this guy has on his fingers? It does not make a word at all, it looks like initials identifying something or other."

Lieutenant Jones said, "Thanks for pointing that out, Jacob. They cleaned the blood that was on his hands. The tattoos did not show before. I wonder if they have any significance. Better make a note of this and ask around. It is very unusual to have tattoos done on your fingers that appear not to mean anything; to us that is."

"Yes, Lieutenant, this is—rather, was—Carl Murdoch. There's enough of him left for me to match the face with the picture I have on his album at home. Sad how a talented man is wasted. Do you have any clue as to why he was murdered in such a way?" Jacob asked.

"Not at the moment Jacob, but I'm sure something will surface somewhere, it always does," concluded the LAPD detective.

## CHAPTER TWO

When Jacob arrived at Claudette Bailey's estate it was just about two p.m. He parked in the circular driveway, got out of the car and began walking to the magnificent oak door. It opened before he could knock and a tall Negro servant asked if he was Mr. Schreiber.

"This is me," Jacob replied. "Is Mrs. Bailey available?"

The servant answered, "Let me take you to the library, sir, and she'll be with you in a moment."

Jacob could not take his eyes off the walls. It was like walking into an art gallery. Painting after painting just hung there. Paintings of all sizes and colors, most looked like originals. As he was guided inside the library room, there were more paintings with thousands of books and what looked like film canisters at one end of the wall, and a diversity of leather chairs and antique sofas. Smack in the middle of it all was the most beautiful massive oak desk, shining like a beacon in the night. The gumshoe thought her husband must spend a lot of time in this very large room. There was even a small bar equipped with sink—counter top and all—next to a large window overlooking what appeared to be a fabulous garden. As Jacob turned at the sound of steps, he saw a tall elegant woman with short white hair and a swing in her walk coming towards him.

"You are right on time, Mr. Schreiber, please do sit down. Would you like to have a cup of tea or coffee?" Claudette Bailey asked.

Jacob answered, "Tea will be fine if that's what you're having. I was just admiring the paintings you have on the walls. So many it must have taken you years to accumulate them. Some of these books in here I have heard about but am seeing for the first time. From the collection of law books I assume your husband is a lawyer, Mrs. Bailey."

Mrs. Bailey said, "Was at one time, became a judge, retired as such, and two years ago had a massive heart attack and died. He was a good man who believed in fairness and justice for all." She rang a bell and when the servant showed up asked to have tea served.

"You mentioned on the telephone this morning that some of your jewelry has been missing. May I ask when you first noticed it?"

"Certainly, Mr. Schreiber. Three days ago a maid by the name of Claire who had been working for me just a short time did not return to work. When I tried to reach her, the telephone number I had for her was no longer in service. I called the employment agency who had referred her to me and they could not reach her either. I am insured for loss but some of the pieces she took had been given to me by my mother who had them given to her by her mother. You can see the sentimental value not to mention the monetary value of these pieces. I would like to recover them without any hassles. When you find this girl, you could offer her money for the return of my jewelry. I'm willing to go as high as ten thousand dollars, Mr. Schreiber."

"How many pieces of jewelry are missing all together?" Jacob asked.

"There are nine in all. Here, I have pictures of the missing pieces marked for easy identification. Take a look for yourself," Mrs. Bailey said.

The servant came in with the sterling silver tray and teapot, deposited it on a small center table and left.

Claudette Bailey said, "I understand you have excellent credentials, Mr. Schreiber. I have prepared a check for you and it's in this envelope. In there as well is the information on Claire Beaumont, at least what I had. The employment agency may have more information on her. I'll call them and ask for their cooperation in this matter. They had better if they wish to do business with me."

Jacob took the envelope from Claudette Bailey. He never bothered looking inside, just placed it in his jacket inside pocket. "I'll look into this for you, Mrs. Bailey. First, I would like a list of all your servants and the hours they work for you. If you don't mind, I would also like to have the opportunity to interrogate them alone and individually. Now why did you not report this to the police?"

"Did I not tell you, Mr. Schreiber? I did, but for insurance purposes only in case you cannot find my jewelry. I don't want any charges brought against Claire Beaumont nor do I want different police officers snooping in my house. This is why I'm hiring you." She then took Jacob upstairs to show him where the jewelry had disappeared from in her private bedroom. Several boxes had been left opened on an immense low profile dresser that resembled the inside of a jewelry counter in a Beverly Hills store.

After another ten minutes of talk, Jacob thanked her and before leaving mentioned that he would be back to talk to the servants within a day or two. As he left the house he couldn't help notice how immaculate the grounds-keeping was. He thought this woman must be filthy rich. Once in the car moving away from the driveway he reached in his left inside pocket and pulled out the envelope she had given him earlier. The check was for twenty thousand dollars. He let out a long whistle. The year was beginning on a positive note.

"Anne, we have a new client, Mrs. Claudette Bailey. Here's a check for deposit. You should see how this woman lives. Did you ever hear of a judge by the name of Richard Nussbaum? He was her husband of thirty years. She was an actress from the silent film era and kept her stage name," Jacob concluded.

Anne said, "I can see by the check she doesn't seem to be in the poor house yet. By the way, George Murdoch called and said he would be here by 4.30. He mentioned he was delayed at a job site in Malibu."

Jacob opened the old file on Peter Murdoch. On his way back he had stopped by the old studio site. There was a notice on the door, which said it would be closed for a week due to a death in the family. *So Peter is still here, just changed his telephone number,* the private eye thought.

Anne knocked on his door to let him know George Murdoch had arrived.

"Good afternoon and my heartfelt sympathies on the loss of your brother Carl. I'm Jacob Schreiber, Mr. Murdoch."

"Thank you, and just call me George, please. I really wanted to meet with you because there are a few things I'm sure the police would never have found out about my brother Carl. He was one hell of a musician but at times, drugs clouded his mind. Not to mention the terrific amount of booze he drank. Carl was a loner. He didn't mind playing in a trio occasionally but really hated the spotlight. In the last few months, he had been involved with some kind of religious group. I know this because he told me about it. My brother said they needed his help. He would record an album and give them the profits. I still don't understand why he did that."

"Was your brother a heavy drug user? By that, I mean did he do it on a regular daily or weekly basis? My other question is about the tattoos on his left hand. Each of the four fingers has a different letter. By the way, George, your brother had my business card in his pocket. Would you know why?"

"Well, Jacob, the letters he had are just like the ones you see here on my left hand. They spell out the first letter of the first name of each brother. We had that done many years ago when Bill, who died in a car crash two years ago, got married. I think Carl had become a regular drug user, he was addicted to cocaine. He made enough money to pay for his habit, did not want to quit. It was killing him. I imagine he got your card from our brother Peter for whom you did some work. The way he was murdered smells of revenge to me. I know he should have never befriended that religious group. They're out on a piece of farmland in Lancaster or near there. The leader's name is Josh and they call themselves the 'Sons of God'. I met this Josh once about three months ago. To me he looked like a freak out of a circus show. The police will most likely say it was a drug deal gone bad, which it appears to be. Trust me, Jacob, my brother Carl was not murdered by a drug dealer. He always had the money to pay for his bad habits. His bank account used to have a balance in the high five figures at all times. It probably still does unless he gave it all away. Carl was not married but had a son out of wedlock. Toby is now twelve and my wife and I have been looking after him since birth. At first, he thought I was his father. As he grew up, we told him my brother Carl was his father. The mother died in childbirth. We only have a few pictures for Toby that his father had given us.

"Here's my address and telephone number where you can reach me. Sometimes I'm hard to get during the day because of the big project I'm working on in Malibu. I'm an architect and civil engineer. After this project, I have two high-rise buildings to design for downtown Los Angeles that will keep me very busy for some time. Is a two thousand dollar retainer sufficient to get you working on finding out who killed my brother, Jacob?"

Jacob said, "It's more than necessary, George. Don't build your hopes up. I may not find the answer you would like to hear. Sometimes a thorough investigation will reveal things that were never known before and be a total disappointment. I'll do my best and will keep in touch. By the way, when do you plan on holding a funeral for Carl?"

"The day after tomorrow, once his body is released to the funeral home," George concluded before leaving the office.

After his client had gone, Jacob handed his secretary the information he had been given and the retainer check. This looked like a busy time ahead for the private investigator. He and Lorraine had found a house in the Woodland Hills sector of the San Fernando Valley. Two acres with good access to Mulholland drive. A bit far to the closest school but Jacob wanted his bride to be a mother to her son Gerald more than a working one. Lorraine could drive her son to school and pick him up at the end of the day. She had—and so had Gerald—agreed to Jacob's suggestion he would legally adopt the boy. He felt it would make it easier for Gerald with other kids. "Children at the age of ten can be cruel to one another," he had said.

*No more walks from the apartment to the office for the time being. Maybe a change in office location would be appropriate.* He was brought out of his daydreaming by Anne who repeatedly was telling him Lieutenant Jones was on the telephone for him.

"Well, Lieutenant, what brings you to my little world at the end of a busy day?" Jacob said as he greeted his friend.

The Lieutenant said, "Are you interested at all in my findings about Carl Murdoch's death? Since he was carrying your card in his pocket he might have wanted you to do some investigative work for him," Jones said.

"The way you say it sounds intriguing. Anything out of the usual, may I ask? Or am I stepping out of line?" Jacob said.

"Not at all Jacob, I offered it. Here's what the autopsy revealed; three bullets from a .45 caliber gun did the damage. The victim had cocaine in his system but the bullets fired at close range are what killed him. In my opinion, Jacob, drug pushers do not carry this kind of handgun. Too heavy and too bulky. Someone who wanted to make sure Mr. Murdoch would not get up and fire back at him did this. I don't have much else to go on at this time. No clues from the bar patrons or members of the trio. Everyone seemed to agree that Carl Murdoch was a good man, a very good musician and a generous person. Everyone said he helped others who were down on their luck. Obviously, he made enough money from the sale of his albums. No wife or children, just two brothers who are both devastated by the violent death of their sibling. I'm going to have to close the file on this one for the time being unless someone comes up with new evidence. How about going to our favorite bar for a before dinner drink?" the homicide detective offered.

"Let's make it a different place, if you don't mind, Lieutenant. You could meet me at the Red Dahlia," Jacob said.

# CHAPTER THREE...

Life does not always go the way one expects it to go. This day happened to be true to form for Jacob Schreiber. He had planned a full day of investigation on the Bailey case. When he called to talk with Claudette Bailey, she told him three of her staff had the day off. She also said that five of the nine missing jewelry pieces, the most valuable ones, had been returned. The gardener had found a small cardboard box near the front door. Jacob had been able to talk to the employment agency that had sent Claire Beaumont to the Bailey's estate a few months back. He located her in South Central Los Angeles. He was to pay her a visit this fine morning, but as he got in his car to start it, the old heap would not budge. Dead battery. By the time he got a new battery put in, he had lost two hours of valuable working time. He got to the area where Ms. Beaumont lived close to noon. The private eye walked up the three steps to the small veranda, badly in need of a coat of paint, and rang the doorbell. A tall Negro woman with eyes frowning answered. Since Jacob did not know what Miss Beaumont looked like, he had to ask for her.

The woman answered, "I'm Claire Beaumont, what is it you want? You look like the police. Are you a detective?" she asked.

"My name is Jacob Schreiber, I'm a private detective, and I was asked by Mrs. Bailey, whom you worked for, to investigate the loss of some jewelry. Would you happen to know anything about it?" Jacob asked Miss Beaumont.

"Are you going to take me to jail, Mr. detective? I already returned some of the old stuff yesterday."

Jacob said, " If you want to give me the other missing pieces right now, I'll give you $500.00 cash and not a word will be said to the police."

The woman appeared to be doing some fast thinking and signaled him to wait right where he was standing. A few minutes later she returned with a small cotton bag.

"Here are the other pieces, I should never had taken them but I thought I could sell them quick. Friends told me they could be traced and I would be caught and end up in jail. Here they are. Do you still give me the money?" Claire Beaumont said.

Jacob took the bag from her, and looked inside to make sure they were the four missing pieces. He went to his pocket, counted five one hundred-dollar bills and handed them to her. "A deal is a deal, Miss Beaumont. There is no need for the police to know about this. I'll make sure Mrs. Bailey understands that."

As he left, he noticed some faces peeking from behind the curtains of the window. The gumshoe knew his client would be happy at the recovery, especially that no damage appeared to have been done to the necklace and three gold bracelets. This had been a fast recovery with a bit of luck attached to it. The day was turning out to be much better than the way it had started. Jacob took the direction of the Palisades and the Bailey's estate. When he arrived there, the former silent film star was taking a walk towards the garden's entrance. She turned around quickly when she saw Jacob getting out of his car.

"Well Mrs. Bailey I have some very good news for you," he said as he handed her the bag containing her missing jewelry. "I do believe this completes my investigation and it only cost me an extra $500.00, which I will deduct from your retainer along with my time and return the difference," the gumshoe concluded.

Mrs. Bailey said, "I will hear none of that kind of talk. Just because you worked fast does not mean you should be paid less. These pieces were all priceless, and the fact you recovered everything without a hassle means a lot to me. Mr. Schreiber, you are an honest and efficient man and I will recommend you to all my friends," said the former film star.

"It was a pleasure to meet you, Mrs. Bailey. and please get yourself a small safe if you don't already have a secured place to hold your valuables. That way, there is less temptation for the servants in the future," Jacob said.

On his way back to the office, Jacob decided to go by The Red Dahlia in West Los Angeles. He walked up to the bartender and identified himself. Jacob wanted to look in the back alley where Carl Murdoch had been found murdered. He knew the LAPD had done an extensive job of taking photographs and dusting for prints.

He was looking for something out of the usual. He looked at every inch from the back door to where the alley ended at a neighborhood street. Nothing seemed to have been overlooked and he decided to return to the bar and have a talk with an employee or two. He was just about to open the back door when he heard a voice say, "Hey, mister, are you looking for something you lost?" said the voice of a young boy.

Jacob turned around to see a nine or ten-year-old looking at him.

"What did you find that could belong to me?" the gumshoe asked.

The boy said, "If you give me two dollars you can have it," as he showed a watch and a small wallet.

"I'll tell you what," Jacob said, "you give me the two items and I'll give you this five dollar bill right here."

The boy took the five and gave Jacob both items. It could be that these items belonged altogether to someone else but the private eye could not take the risk. He thought that perhaps the watch and/or the wallet had been Carl Murdoch's property. He opened the back door and re-entered The Red Dahlia. The bartender was a talkative type person and volunteered information that was not relevant to the murder investigation. Jacob ordered a beer and listened attentively. Then the bartender said, "I just remembered a couple of weeks ago Carl came in here with an odd couple. The woman was a tall 5'8" redhead about thirty years old. The guy was shorter than her by at least an inch, bald and about forty. Their conversation, what I could hear of it, was animated and focused on music. I also noticed the bald guy was smoking a pipe. There were many arguments while they sat and drank beer for about an hour. The girl was the aggressive one. I got busy and the next time I looked Carl and the girl were gone. The bald guy stayed until some fellow with long brown hair came in, had a beer with him and then the two of them left together. I had never seen these people before nor have I seen them since Carl was killed. I think I overheard them talk about some kind of religious group."

Jacob thanked him for the information and left the bar for the office. Hollywood Boulevard is a busy place at any time of the day, what with tourists hoping to run into some movie stars and wannabes looking to be found! It could be classified as a combination of the good, the bad and the lost soul. Jacob, in his usual manner, ran up the two flight of stairs leading to his second floor office.

As he walked into his office, Anne said, "Jacob I have several messages for you. Mrs. Bailey, George Murdoch and Lieutenant Jones. Then the campaign office for the DA wants to know if you would like to buy some tickets for a political dinner two weeks from tomorrow. They're $25.00 each and the dinner will be held at the Wilshire Country Club," as she handed her boss the messages.

"Thanks Anne, don't know what I would do without you. By the way, you can put a closure to the Bailey case. All missing jewelry has been found and returned to its owner. For accounting purposes you can count four days of work plus my expenses and office overhead," the private eye said. He went to his desk and placed the messages down.

First, he would call George Murdoch. "Jacob Schreiber here, Mr. Murdoch, returning your call. So, the police have been questioning you. Anything in particular they wanted to know? I understand the reasoning behind the questions. They obviously don't have a clue as to why your brother was brutally murdered. Do you think you could stop by my office before the end of the day? I have a couple of items I would like to show you. Good, see you later." Jacob realized that George was the one closer to Carl. Peter may have been the other musical hand in the family but age-wise George and Carl were much closer. They shared a lot more with each other. Jacob took the watch and small wallet out of his pockets and placed them on his desk. He would soon find out if they belonged to brother Carl.

"Lieutenant, this is Jacob, you called earlier today, anything I can do for you like solving a murder or something?" the gumshoe said with a smile in his voice.

The Lieutenant answered, "How about nine or ten of them. I can't pay you what you get privately, but I'll give you all the support you need," Bill Jones answered in a jesting manner. "I've come up against a brick wall on this Murdoch case. I seem to be at a dead-end. One of my boys said he saw you near The Red Dahlia earlier. Did you find anything that would help this investigation move forward instead of going nowhere? You know, Jacob, when the trail cools off fast, it makes it extremely difficult for us to find any clues that would help lead us to a conclusion. I was hoping you may have something to pass on to me," the homicide detective concluded.

"You must have read my mind, Bill," Jacob said. "I may have something after I meet with my client

George Murdoch, brother of deceased Carl. He hired me to help find anything that would help you, the police, move faster towards a closure. He should be in my office in the next hour. I'll call you back after my meeting with him. Anything else you would like, my friend? Good, then I'll be talking to you soon Lieutenant," said the private eye.

Jacob just sat there, thinking about Carl Murdoch. The young boy in the alley had told him where in the garbage bin he had found the watch and wallet. The bartender suddenly remembered two people not mentioned before. Amongst all that there has to be a clue of some kind leading towards the responsible party to the murder. Tomorrow he would take a drive towards Lancaster and see if he could locate this Josh and his band of merry men.

Anne peeked in the door to let him know she was leaving and not to forget to call Lorraine after he was done with his client. It had to do with the upcoming little league season, she had said.

George Murdoch arrived ahead of time. They both sat there and chitchatted until Jacob showed him the watch and the wallet.

"The watch looks familiar to me, George said, but I can't say for certain. The wallet was Carl's. The two photos in there are of my kids. He was godfather to my oldest boy Carl, whom we named after him. Is that all there was in the wallet? How about his driver's license, it should have been in there too. I know he always carried money with him, what about that, Mr. Schreiber?" said the devastated brother.

Jacob said, "Sometimes a hitman who does not want to be found will take most everything out of a victim's wallet to make it look like a robbery. It has happened in many other cases I've been on. May I keep the watch and the wallet for the time being, Mr. Murdoch? Tomorrow I have another avenue I'm going to pursue and when I have more evidence I will let you know."

Murdoch left and Jacob thought that maybe tomorrow would bring some light in this dark tunnel. He picked up the telephone and dialed Lorraine's number.

## CHAPTER FOUR...

Jacob's drive to Lancaster had not been success-ful. It took him two hours to locate where this Josh character and his followers were living. Some ten miles outside of Lancaster he finally located "The Sons of God." They appeared to be a rather reclusive group of people. There was a locked gate on the other side of which were two guard dogs and a young man with a rifle in his hands. Obviously, these people did not want intruders or anyone snooping around. He told Jacob that Josh, their leader, was not there at the moment and would not be back for a couple of days. As Jacob returned to his car, he no-ticed a couple of people on horseback coming to-wards the man at the gate. He couldn't hear what they were saying but saw the young man he had spoken to point in his direction. The two riders looked, turned around and went back towards the hill where the ranch house seemed to be located.

On his way back to the office, many thoughts went through his mind. Now, why would a religious group have guard dogs and armed guards? There must be something else going on at the ranch they didn't want other people to see. Jacob entered his office building in his usual stride, running up the stairs to his second floor work compound. The old elevator was still not working at full speed.

Anne handed him some telephone messages for him to look after.

Jacob made the first call to his LAPD friend Lieutenant Jones. "This is Jacob returning your call, Lieutenant. Anything special going on? By the way I have something I ran into today you may want to look at. Why don't we get together for a beer at the end of the day and I'll fill you in."

Lieutenant Jones answered, "It sounds good to me, Jacob. Why don't we make it closer to six at our usual place on Wilshire Boulevard?"

Jacob knew he would need the help of his friend eventually if he wanted to find out about The sons of God. There appeared to be more to this group than a religious slant.

The second call was to the bartender at The Red Dahlia. "Chuck, this is Jacob Schreiber, you called earlier today. Anything I can do for you, my friend?" the gumshoe asked.

The bartender said, "Why don't you come by when you have a moment, Jacob, I have more information concerning Carl Murdoch for you."

In the private investigating business, you never know where the clues may come from. Jacob had always made it a policy to befriend bartenders and waiters. They encountered many people and overheard interesting conversations at times. As a source of free information, they were the most reliable. He decided to strike while the iron was hot. The private eye left the office, got in his car and drove to West LA where The Red Dahlia was located.

He arrived at his rendezvous with the Lieutenant some twenty minutes late. "I see you didn't expect me to show up again, no beer for me." Just as he sat down the waiter deposited his favorite beverage on the table, compliments of the Lieutenant.

The information Jacob got from the bartender at The Red Dahlia was in a way off-track. Yet, he had his best opportunity for feedback with the head of Homicide. "As I said to you Lieutenant, I have some information that may send you in a totally different direction in Carl Murdoch's murder case. For example, he had been seen in the past two to three months in the company of a guy by the name of Josh. This fellow is apparently the leader of a religious group who call themselves 'The Sons of God' and either own or lease a ranch some ten miles out of Lancaster in the high desert. I went there earlier today. To my surprise, the gate was locked. On the other side of this gate were two ferocious guard dogs and a young man in some kind of dirty gray, long robe holding a high powered rifle in his hands. Now that's only the beginning, Bill," Jacob said.

"That far up north is out of my jurisdiction. Either the Sheriff or Highway Patrol can go in there if they have a reason to believe some illegal activities are going on. They would most likely require proof of some kind before they make a move. On the other hand, I don't know how our FBI friend. Remember Special Agent Paul Trickten? He would take to going in somewhere unannounced without something to fall back on. For what you are saying, those are the only suggestions I have right now, the LAPD detective concluded.

Jacob said, "I just came back from The Red Dahlia, my reason for being late, where one of the bartenders told me about a very interesting conversation he overheard a few days ago. It seems that this Josh individual—who makes himself look like pictures of Jesus Christ—is not so ceremoniously religious. In his choice of words, when having a beer with some guy dressed like the picture gallery in a Mafia yearend book, did not sound Christian-like to the bartender Your mention of the FBI is very appropriate, Lieutenant. Why is it that I don't seem to be able to work on a straight murder case? You know the old saying about criminals being unable to keep their mouths shut is very revealing. This Josh fellow was talking to his drinking partner about plates in denominations of 20's, 50's and 100's. They obviously are either printing or looking to print illegal bills. Counterfeiting I believe is a Federal offence, therefore, FBI jurisdiction. Chuck—the bartender—told me he overheard the Mafia look-alike character tell Josh that Uncle Vito would have to approve. I assume he meant Vito Profacini, our resident Southern California godfather. Again, this is a very interesting twist to a murder that first appeared to be motivated by theft. What do you think about this? Have there been any complaints of counterfeit money in circulation within your district lately? Was Carl Murdoch involved in this scam?"

The Lieutenant said, "I haven't heard of any. Just the same, I must tell you counterfeiting is not under my command. It doesn't mean that it's not happening though. I'll have to check with the fraud squad in the morning. Very interesting what you are telling me about this group. What did you call them, The Sons of God? I guess they figured there had to be some other way to pass the collection plate around. Did you not tell me you had some other information related to the Murdoch's case, you wanted to talk about?" concluded the detective.

The talking seemed to have made Jacob thirsty, he ordered two more beers before going into his pocket to bring out what he had obtained from the kid in the back alley of The Red Dahlia. For some reason when Jacob got involved either directly or indirectly in the investigation of a specific murder, other things always crawled to the surface. Things of a different nature!

"Yes, Lieutenant, I do have something to show you," Jacob said. He reached in his pocket and pulled out an old worn leather wallet and a wristwatch with a black leather band. "These two items—according to my source—were found in one of the garbage bins at the rear of the bar where Carl Murdoch was killed. His brother George already identified the wallet as being Carl's. Two photographs inside are George's kids. He was not sure about the wristwatch although it looked familiar to him. What's interesting in here, Lieutenant, is the missing driver's license or any other form of ID a person usually carries on himself. I know from the brothers that Carl belonged to the musicians' union. You would think that an ID of such value would be in a person's wallet," Jacob said.

"It's interesting that you should come across evidence of this sort when my men searched that alley back and forth without finding these items. Did you find these or did someone give them to you Jacob."

Jacob answered, "It was a ten year-old kid who sold them to me for five bucks when he saw me searching the alley. Just got lucky I guess."

"I'm glad this is the way it happened, otherwise I would have to reprimand some of my crew. May I take these with me as evidence? Like you said, it seems unusual for someone not to have any Ids in their wallet. It may be that whoever killed Carl Murdoch took the Ids out to make it look like a theft. At least, that's what I think for now, Jacob."

"We're riding on the same train, Lieutenant. I also think the missing Ids were done on purpose to get the investigators off the right track. I think the FBI might find an incentive once I talk to Special Agent Paul Trickten. The Sons of God should be of interest to him especially if Vito Profacini is in the background of this operation," Jacob concluded.

The two friends parted company. The gumshoe had to go to a little league meeting concerning the scheduling for the new season. By the time he got home, it was after 10 PM. He got a beer from the refrigerator, sat down and called his fiancée. Lorraine was in a good mood. Her sister Colette had been over for dinner and looked to be doing well after that terrible accident she had last fall. Jacob told her about wanting to go look for a house this coming Saturday. He thought the Toluca Lake area or Burbank would be nice, a good comparison with Woodland Hills. The discussion went on about schooling for Gerald and what area would be best for him. In his conversations with Lorraine, Jacob avoided business talk. There were times when the business side of things was not so pleasant, so he kept it to himself.

Jacob said, "How would you like to have lunch with me tomorrow? We could go to the Wilshire Country Club... Good, I'll pick you up in front of your work place shortly after noon." After he hung up he took a hot shower and went straight to bed.

The constant ringing of the telephone woke him. "What!" He said to himself, "5.30 a.m. Who in the world could be calling at this time? It had better be good." Jacob picked up the telephone, "Schreiber here."

There was a slight pause and then the Lieutenant's voice came out loud and clear. "Sorry to bother you so early, Jacob, but I have a corpse here you would be interested in. It was discovered after four this morning when the cleaner came into The Red Dahlia."

By now, Jacob was wide-awake.

"Do you know who it is, Lieutenant?" the gumshoe asked.

"From the Ids we found on him it appears to be Chuck Long, the bartender you mentioned yesterday. I'll be here for another hour or so should you decide to come and identify this guy for me," the Lieutenant concluded.

Jacob got up, dressed and was out the door in no time flat. When he arrived at The Red Dahlia a young officer stopped him before he recognized the private eye. Everyone on the force knew about the friendship between Schreiber, the private investigator, and Jones, the Homicide Lieutenant. They knew if Jacob was there, someone had called him.

"Well, Jacob, this time the body did not have your business card but because you mentioned him yesterday I thought you should be in on this from the very beginning," the detective said. "Would you look at the body and tell me if it is the guy you spoke to yesterday?"

Jacob came over behind the bar where the body was laid out on its back. The man had been shot several times in the chest. "Yes Lieutenant, it is Chuck Long to whom I spoke yesterday. Someone must have overheard my conversation with him and decided this was a risk that had to be eliminated immediately. Aside from the bullet holes in his chest, are there any other clues, anything left close to the body?" asked the private detective.

"Well Jacob, if you bend down closer to the body you will notice the victim tried to write something on the door of the cooler. It looks like the beginning of numbers, but hard to tell as I can only guess he expired before he could complete his message," the head of homicide said.

Jacob got closer to the corpse and came back up quickly. "Lieutenant, look at this closely. What he was trying to write looks like the first two numbers of my office telephone exchange. He was trying to give us a clue about the hitman," Jacob concluded.

Lieutenant Jones bent down to look at the door again and then called the police photographer to register this new evidence. "It does look like he was trying to write numbers and the first two look like your office exchange. I guess the poor bastard died before he could complete the next number." The police Lieutenant turned to Jacob, "Thanks for noticing that, my friend. I'm sure it has some significance attached to it," Bill Jones concluded.

**CHAPTER FIVE...**

Jacob Schreiber decided that today was a day to make amends. He made an appointment to meet with Helen Billings at her home. He wanted her to know he had secured the items from the bank deposit box her former husband had concealed. The papers found in that box had helped the FBI put a stop to the theft of military weapons and their sale to foreign countries. A billion dollar business. It also helped incarcerate some heavy Mafia members. All that was fine but what bothered him was the cash amount he had found and placed in a secure account. Seventy-five thousand dollars—minus his fee and the replacement of his office furniture, damages totaling around twenty-five thousand—Jacob was ready to return the difference.

Helen had moved to a new home in Toluca Lake, a two-acre property with a large garden and well fenced. When Jacob arrived, she had tea and biscuits ready, a dramatic change from her drinking days. "Well Jacob, you seem surprised, don't you like tea?" Helen asked.

"You bet I do, Helen, but, tell me .is this a new trend? And if it is, I'm happy for you. You really look wonderful, healthy, and may I say, wiser," said the private eye. "You partly know why I'm here but let me explain to you the part I had not told you before, or anyone else for that matter." Jacob went on to tell Helen how he had found the safety deposit box at a bank in Beverly Hills. He explained about the cash he had found and the purpose he had in mind for keeping it. The gumshoe told his former client about the many cases he took on a pro-bono basis. "You see Helen my real purpose was to help people who legitimately could not pay for my services or any other private investigators. That money would serve the poor with no questions asked."

Helen interrupted him for a moment. "Jacob, you found for me several million dollars I would never have known existed and would have been seized by the government had you not secured the bank books. Please don't mention this anymore. Any little amount you may have kept, you deserve to have. If it had not been for you, the police and the FBI would have never been able to find who was behind the military weapons thefts. You did the whole country a great service. Use this small amount of cash whichever way you want. Now let me tell you about me," Helen said.

She told Jacob how a dear friend made her realize she was drinking too much. At first, it was not easy but with the help of her friend and a determination to feel better, she had finally succeeded in stopping her drinking altogether. Now she was involved in helping young artists pursue their careers by funding a special school program for them. "It is very rewarding," she concluded.

Some twenty minutes later Jacob left with a spring in his walk and a burden lifted off his shoulders. His conscience was at peace and he could go on doing with the money what he had first intended to do with it.

When he arrived at his office, Anne immediately handed him some telephone messages he had received. He noticed one was from George Murdoch, one from his LAPD friend Lieutenant Jones, and a third one from a Don P. Ryle, special agent with the FBI. This last one would be the first call he would make.

"Jacob Schreiber, returning a call from Special Agent Ryle."

The telephone receptionist told him to hold for a moment, and then a voice with a slight southern accent came on.

"Let me introduce myself," the man said. "Mr. Schreiber, my associate Paul Trickten has been promoted to Washington DC. I'm the new kid in town and would like very much to meet with you. Paul told me so many good things about you, I just want to make sure he wasn't under the influence when he met you," agent Ryle said with a smile in his tone.

"It sounds good to me, Mr. Ryle. By the way you can call me Jacob, it won't make me feel so old. How about getting together for lunch today? The treat's on me. Do you know where the Wilshire Country Club is? Good, meet me there, shall we say 12.30, if it's okay with you," concluded a surprised private eye.

His second call was to George Murdoch who had wanted to inform him he had found some interesting notes in a book found at Carl's former apartment. It concerned The Sons of God and the purposes of their activities. Jacob told him he would get it from him later in the day.

Then his last call. "Jacob here, Lieutenant, got something new for me?"

"Yes and no, Jacob. We have been getting some complaints about some freaks standing on street corners downtown and begging. I thought I recognized one of them, but no, it was just a resemblance to one of my contacts. I checked around with the fraud squad but so far no report of bogy bills of any denomination circulating around. It may be that these Sons of God are not ready to distribute the money just yet! Do you have anything on your side of the hill?" Bill Jones asked.

"It just happens I may have later today. I'm just waiting for a source to show up. By the way, did you know Paul Trickten had been promoted and transferred to the Nation's Capital? We have a new man in his place. Let's see, I have his name written here. Got it, a Donald Peter Ryle is now the special agent in charge of the FBI here in Los Angeles. Sounds like a nice guy. I'm having lunch with him today. He called me as a courtesy to Paul. That's what I call starting a relationship on the right foot, wouldn't you say?" Jacob said.

Lieutenant Jones said, "I heard about this guy. Used to be a New York cop and when the war ended joined the FBI. I believe he was an Air Force major. Good luck at your lunch meeting. Don't forget to let me know what your source had for you."

Jason quickly looked at his file on Murdoch and walked to Anne's desk with it. He pulled out an envelope from his pocket and handed it to his secretary with the file.

"Is this envelope to be placed in the file Jacob?" she asked.

"Read the content you'll know where to file it then," he said with a grin on his face.

"When I see you smile like that," Anne said, "I know you've been up to something," as she pulled out the one sheet from the envelope. "Oh! I see," as she read the note given to Jacob by Helen Billings in regards to the $75K. "Must be your lucky Friday. I'm glad for us. Now we don't have to be concerned about questions being asked from anywhere. While you were on the telephone, a Don Ryle called. He said he was to have lunch with you and asked to make it a half-hour later. Is this the new FBI man in LA?"

"He is, Anne, and sounds like a real nice person. It will be worth my time to establish a good rapport with him. You know, it makes it easier when we have to deal with investigations touching the federal jurisdiction," Jacob said. "I'm going to need him on the Murdoch case. Looks like those Christian fellows are not so Christian-like after all."

Anne said, "You haven't told me anything about your trip to Lancaster yet. Did something happened there to make you say what you just said?"

"How about armed guards and ferocious dogs and a locked gate at what is supposed to be 'a prayer place' for the converted. There is more going on there than meets the eye. In fact, you cannot see any buildings from where the gate stands. Did I not tell you about Chuck, one of the bartenders at The Red Dahlia in West LA, who was murdered I presume, after he was overheard talking to me? I have notes on my desk for you to place in the Murdoch file. Soon everything will fall into place," the gumshoe concluded.

"Before I forget, Lorraine also called earlier to let you know she will be at the practice field tonight. She thought you could all go for hotdogs after."

"Thanks for reminding me Anne, I almost forgot about it. Better get my thinking done before I meet the big man from the FBI." Jacob sat at his desk and thought about the events since Carl Murdoch had been murdered. There were still some missing pieces to the puzzle, but they would soon be located. He had to convince this new special agent to search the compound where Josh and his disciples of God were temporarily living.

His meeting with the new FBI special agent went well. Jacob was sure Don would act soon on The Sons of God out of Lancaster. Once he got the notebook from George Murdoch he would look at it, then turn it over to the FBI for action. As a private investigator, he felt that going it alone in this case would not be proper. Counterfeiting, if there was, fell under the Feds who were well equipped to handle it.

He took a drive to Malibu where Murdoch was working on a building project, secured the book from him and returned to his office. Jacob just went through the book page after page and found some twenty pages, which could be of interest to the FBI. They contained information on where the fake bills would be passed and how many each time. There were places in the four corners of the greater Los Angeles area as well as Orange County and San Diego. Most places were affluent areas with expensive merchandise. The whole 'campaign' was to begin in early spring when there were still many tourists around.

The last three pages were the most interesting ones. In them, Carl Murdoch named the drug pushers he knew of, the source of the drugs and how these people could be reached. He mentioned that Josh had approached him to control a group of 'money pushers' but he had refused. In the last page, he mentions the threats he received and what they would do to his family if he did not cooperate now that he knew so much.

Jacob just sat there shaking his head. He figured Carl had asked his brother for the card a day or two before he was murdered. This book was quite a revelation and would add strength to the story he had already given the FBI. Surveillance in this case was an impossibility unless they could infiltrate the group. That was up to the special agent to decide. Interesting he thought.

He handed the book to Anne and asked her to copy about twenty-four pages of it, make an extra copy for Lieutenant Jones and secure them in the safe. George Murdoch had told Jacob he had had a look at the content of the notebook but could not make head nor tail out of it. He was hoping the private eye would, since investigation was his line of work.

The gumshoe concluded that someone in the criminal organization of Profacini or possibly this Josh individual was afraid Carl Murdoch would spill the beans on them. This gave them a reason for a quick elimination. To leave the body close to his hangout had certainly not been a good idea. Again maybe Carl did not want to go quietly so in a moment of panic the hitman completed his contract.

Anne came in to tell him Lieutenant Jones was on the telephone.

"Well, Lieutenant, you caught me red-handed. Here I am sitting in my office doing absolutely nothing but some thinking. What can I do for you?" Jacob asked.

"First you could tell me how your lunch went with the new FBI man. Then I will tell you what we located today in a garbage bin two blocks away from The Red Dahlia," the homicide detective said.

Jacob answered, "The meeting went well. My feeling is that I convinced Ryle about the counterfeiting operation. Now that I have this book on hand, I can confirm it. By the way, I have a copy put aside for you. So what did you find while snooping in the garbage?"

"Thanks for filling me in on Ryle. What we found Jacob is the .45 gun that killed Murdoch. The ballistic test was conclusive. The gun had been reported stolen from a store in Santa Monica some three weeks ago. No prints were left on it, and we don't know who stole it. The storeowner thinks it was some guy with long hair who came in to buy ammunition for shot guns and rifles. They were four together and they chose a time when no other customers were in the store. Two of them were interested in some guns he had on display on a wall at the end of the store. From the description you gave me of this Josh, I think it was him and his gang, but to prove it is another story," the Lieutenant concluded.

"Come by tomorrow, we'll have coffee," Jacob said.

**CHAPTER SIX...**

After the last practice, Jacob had taken the whole team for hotdogs and drinks. He felt it gave the boys a sense of team togetherness. It was good for the morale and created an atmosphere of friendship amongst the parents, too. That Friday night he had found Lorraine's mood different. He didn't know what to make of it but would wait for the first opportunity to find out.

She had come to the ballpark with her sister, a friend of Colette by the name of Joan, and her brother Rick. Nothing unusual there he thought, and decided not to fret on it. He did find Lorraine's behavior somewhat different but made nothing of it. When she told him she would talk to him tomorrow, a warning light went on. Still he had too much on his mind to worry about something that may not even be there. He would have a talk with her tomorrow and find out what was bothering her. They set up a time to meet at ten o'clock at Jacob's apartment.

The next morning Lorraine arrived on time. When Jacob went to give her a hug and a kiss, she shrugged away.

"What seems to be the problem, Lorraine, why the cold shoulder?" Jacob asked.

Lorraine said, "It has nothing to do with you, Jacob, it's me. I don't want to get married to you now or at anytime. Rick whom you saw last night was my high school sweetheart and we still have strong feelings for each other. I'm sorry but I cannot help it. Here I brought your ring back."

Jacob was taken by surprise. "When did you decide on this move, may I ask? Last week, two weeks ago or has it been in your plans for a long time?" He sounded hurt and was holding back. It was not his habit to shout or get angry. The private eye always had a grip on his emotions. This time he found it tough but held on. "What about Gerald, is he aware of what you are doing?" Jacob said.

"My boy will adjust, he likes Rick too. We are going to move to San Diego where he has his law practice," Lorraine said. "He handles a general law practice with a specialty in family law. I plan to move this coming week. My sister has also found work with a new firm in La Jolla. I'm sorry, Jacob, but I just have to do this. You've been good to me and especially to Gerald by taking him on your baseball team. The work you do scares me at times and I couldn't live with that. It's enough that I lost a husband in the war. I have to go now," Lorraine concluded as she walked towards the door.

Jacob did not try to stop her, he knew better. He wished her good luck. This was no time for deploying emotions. It would be hard on him but he'd get over it. His work was always his first priority anyway. He figured the fatherless boy had drawn him towards the mother. *Life must go on* he muttered to himself. Saturdays had been for socializing lately, but today he would go to the office and search through his current files for possible new clues. He made himself some bacon and eggs, had a cup of coffee then left.

The file on Carl Murdoch contained some information about drug dealers and the counterfeit operation outside of Lancaster. Maybe in there somewhere he would find a clue, which would help him move forward. The ringing of his telephone startled him. "Jacob Schreiber here," said the private eye in a lower tone than normal.

"I'm glad I caught you there, Jacob. This is Don Ryle of the FBI. Could I come to see you right now? I have something I would like to talk over with you, if it's convenient," said the special agent.

"Absolutely, Don, I'll go downstairs and get us a coffee. See you soon," Jacob said. *I wonder what he has in mind. My mention of Josh and his sons of God living in a well-guarded compound probably got the best of his curiosity. When he gets here, I'll find out.*

FBI special agent Don P. Ryle arrived with a briefcase and a smile on his face.

"You look like the cat who swallowed the canary," Jacob said.

"It all depends on you, Jacob," said the Federal man. "I have a judge convinced, if I can bring him any small evidence, to issue a general search warrant for this property out Lancaster way. I hope you have some kind of address or good direction as to its location. When I do, I'll take ten men with me. You're welcome to come along," said the special agent.

"Here's a coffee for you. Let me get you a notebook given to me yesterday by George Murdoch. He found it in his brother's personal affairs and thought I could use the information contained in it." Jacob went to his wall safe and got the book in question.

"Here it is, Don, I was going to give it to you on Monday but you beat me to it. I marked the pages that could be of interest to you, as you can see. You can keep it. I made copies of the pages I may need for future references. I'm sure Lieutenant Jones will be glad to find the local drug pushers without any hassle. By the way, have you met Bill Jones yet?"

Don Ryle answered, "Late yesterday. I had the pleasure to do so at a reception the Chief of Police and the Mayor were holding. My first impression is very positive and he seems to like you a lot. He mentioned that you served in the South Pacific under his brother's command. Yes, this little book will do the trick with the judge on Monday."

They chitchatted for a while then the special agent said, "I just want you to know that if you need my cooperation at any time, it's there for you. I know I can count on yours. Tomorrow afternoon we're having a Bar-B-Q at our house and you're welcome to come over if you can."

"Sounds good to me, Don, I'll bring some beer along. Any special brand you would like?" Jacob asked.

"No," Don said, "just bring whatever you want. Maybe we can talk about this ranch and the people in it tomorrow. Four of my men will be there, too. You'll have a chance to meet them beforehand, if you haven't already."

Jacob said, "You had better come prepared. What I saw at the gate was not meant to be a friendly reception. We may also run into some of Profacini's boys since I feel they're involved in this project. I don't have any proof, aside from what Carl Murdoch wrote in that book, concerning an illegal operation of some kind going on. Logic would say you don't need guard dogs and armed personnel if you are doing a legitimate business. Someone in that group killed Carl Murdoch because they feared he would spill the beans on them. Then that someone or another member of the group overheard my conversation with Chuck Long, the bartender, and sent him to the Promised Land. The Red Dahlia has become a dangerous place to be seen in. The sooner we move, the better life will be. Thanks for the invitation, Don, I'll be there around 4.30 tomorrow."

The special agent left Jacob's office with the notebook secured in his briefcase. The private eye was pleased he had been invited to participate in the search. Now, to his knowledge, this had never happened before. *A private investigator being asked by the FBI to come along with them on a mission, probably a first.* He realized his relationship was strong. His credibility with different law enforcement agencies had never been in question. Jacob Schreiber was known as a straight shooter, a no-nonsense person who would bend the rules when he needed to but cooperate even when not asked to do so. As a private investigator, Jacob felt it was important to have friends in different agencies. These contacts helped speed up an investigation. He knew that, they knew that, and everyone was comfortable with the situation. The telephone rang to take him away from his thoughts.

"Schreiber Investigation," Jacob said.

A muffled voice said, "Listen, Schreiber, you don't need to know who this is but I'd like to send a friendly warning your way. Quit poking your nose in Carl Murdoch's affairs. The next call will be a bullet through your head."

The telephone went dead before Jacob could say anything.

*Now that was not very friendly,* he thought. Threats on his life had happened many times at the beginning of an investigation. He must be on the right track for someone to phone in the threat. Jacob did not intend to quit his investigation. Threats of this nature just gave him more incentive to find the culprits. He would have to be a bit more vigilant and aware of his surroundings for the time being.

The B-B-Q party at Ryle's house was a relaxing time for Jacob. He got the opportunity to meet a couple of the new agents recently assigned to Los Angeles. To his surprise, Lieutenant Jones was also there and Jacob chose the moment to tell him about the telephone threat from the previous day.

"Well, Lieutenant, did you have a chance to thoroughly go through the pages from Murdoch's notebook?" the gumshoe asked.

"I did, Jacob. My colleagues in Narcotics and in Fraud were impressed and pleased to have this kind of information. Again, I made sure to let them know where it came from. A little back-slapping now and then doesn't hurt, just in case you ever need their cooperation. I heard from our host that you are going to be part of the group when they go up to Lancaster in a day or two. You made the right move by giving Ryle the book. If anyone can do something about this supposedly religious group, they can," concluded the homicide detective.

Jacob was pleased at accepting the invitation from special agent Ryle. It had given him the opportunity to meet some of the essential players around the new FBI boss.

Later that evening when he was home listening to the late news on the radio he mentally went through the whole B-B-Q scenario. Ryle had also chosen the occasion to do some public relations himself. It gave him the idea that once a month they should get together in some unofficial fashion. His thoughts went back to Saturday morning and Lorraine's surprise decision. He was somewhat disturbed by it, but not to a point of distress. She had made the choice and he respected that. *Better now than later,* he thought.

He had his eye on a property he had seen in the Encino area. This coming week he would ask his secretary, Anne Dombrowski, to have a look at the place with him. It might just be the right time for him to pick up some real estate. Tomorrow was another day. He turned off the lights and went to bed.

He arrived at his office a bit later than usual. Anne had some telephone messages waiting for him. There was his usual friendly call from his friend at the LAPD homicide division. Two others he did not recognize the names, so he would start with them first. "Jacob Schreiber here, Mr. Plant, I'm returning your call," the gumshoe said.

"I'm James Plant, Mr. Schreiber, and the reason I called you is because I have had some problem with disappearing merchandise from my warehouse. You see, I operate a transitional warehouse and hold shipments in transit from customs. I know you're going to say, 'why don't I get the FBI to investigate'. I went that route and was told that because I'm a private contractor and not a government facility as such, they have no authority to investigate," concluded the businessman.

"How about if I come to see you in about an hour, Mr. Plant? Would that be suitable for you? Good I'll see you then and we can discuss whether I can be of service to you or not." Jacob thought how amazing it was that new clients kept popping up. He was sure someone had referred this last man to him.

"Well, Lieutenant, you're up bright and early. Was the City of Angels in a heavenly mood overnight or did she take a walk with the devil?" Jacob said with a smile in his voice.

"You are quite poetic so early in the day. Did you ever think of changing profession and become a writer? It might be easier on your social life, my friend," said the Lieutenant. "On a more serious note, we do have a new development overnight. My colleagues from Narcotics arrested a Grant Smith following a tip received and the help of Murdoch's notebook. Smith has agreed to give them information on the counterfeiting operation in Lancaster and possibly the murder of Carl Murdoch. All this in exchange for no jail time. We should have more by the end of the day. We're going to let the FBI in on this one. It may be beneficial for all of us. Just thought I'd keep you informed," said a happy detective.

"This is good news, Lieutenant. Any chance I could talk to this Smith fellow after the narcotic squad is done with him? Let me know if you can arrange it for me. I'll owe you one in this case." After he hung up Jacob left for San Pedro to meet with James Plant.

## CHAPTER SEVEN...

The telephone kept on ringing and Jacob rushed out of the shower to answer, wondering who could be calling at this time of the evening.

"Schreiber here," he answered in a professional tone. "Well good evening to you too, Don. Anything special on your mind? By the way thanks again for the invite yesterday. I was able to meet a couple of your men I had not met before."

"Well, Jacob, I have the search warrant for the Lancaster compound. We are planning on showing up there at 5 a.m. Are you still wanting to come along with us or do you want to pass on it and await the results?" said the special FBI agent.

"Just tell me where to meet you and I'll be there. Good, see you at your headquarters at 3.30 a.m.," the gumshoe said. *These guys move fast for Federal agents*, Jacob thought. He set his alarm and went to bed for a short night, but he thought it would be worth it.

When Jacob arrived at the Federal building he noticed the third floor lights were mostly all on. As he got in, a security guard checked his ID and told him where he would find Mr. Ryle. As a former junior officer in the Marines, he knew how to behave with the Federal agency. Having been invited to participate instead of him asking was the whole difference. When he walked in, Special Agent Ryle walked over to greet him.

Don Ryle called everyone to pay attention. "Gentlemen, this is Jacob Schreiber, a special private investigator. Most of you know him and for those who don't, let's just say he's like one of us. I have invited him to be with us today because without him we would not have known about this group until a lot of damage would have been done. For the purpose of this exercise we are going to divide ourselves in groups of four." Ryle pointed to two young agents and said, "You two are going to be with Schreiber and me. The rest of you can form your own team. Remember gentlemen, these people are armed with high-powered rifles and god knows what else. They are, as far as I'm concerned, extremely dangerous. We have to exercise caution. If possible, we hope to prevent any casualty. By the time we get there, it will be daylight. Any questions anyone would like to ask? Good, then, we leave in ten minutes," concluded the special agent as he invited Jacob to follow him.

When they got to the gate of the ranch, it was locked. One of the agents pulled out a pair of heavy steel cutters and they were able to proceed right in.

It had all been decided to leave the cars by the gate and the men would proceed on foot. Two of the front agents had tranquilizer guns and had to use them as the dogs came towards them. Since they hadn't barked, no one from the house they could see, was out of bed. High brush along the walk helped to camouflage the group from the front porch view. There was also a barn some 150 yards from the main house, and a couple of small shacks that looked like outhouses. They could also see a well in the background. As they got closer they decided to split, surround the house and cover the barn at the same time. Ryle was thinking that his choice of twenty-four men was just the right number for the operation. As they inched closer to the steps of the house, they saw a man sitting in a rocking chair with a rifle between his knees.

One of the agents got within three feet of the guard before he woke up with a surprised look on his face. The agent hit him hard enough to knock him out but not before he could pull the trigger on his rifle. The sound was deafening and they were sure the whole house would be awakened by it.

Not knowing how many were in the house, they rushed in like a military combat unit. Three men had been sleeping downstairs and were immediately handcuffed and their guns pulled away.

An agent at the bottom of the stairs yelled, "FBI, come down with your hands on top of your head." They heard the shuffle of feet, the breaking of glass where someone tried to escape through a window. That one was shot in the legs and fell to the ground where two agents secured him. Once they had rushed the house, the whole operation took less than two minutes to complete.

At the house seven men were apprehended. The group of agents who had gone to the barn reported no one on the premises. A tall young man with a beard growth that almost reached his shoulders shouted, "Who the hell are you people and what is it you want?"

Don Ryle said, "First of all, tell me if you are the leader of this group. We are the FBI and I hold a Federal search warrant for this place," as he waved it in front of the man's face.

"I'm Josh, the leader. Let me look at this piece of paper you so defiantly wave at me." Josh was given the warrant and read it slowly and carefully. "You must be crazy to barge in here like leftover commandos from the Second World War. There is no," and he looked at the warrant again, "counterfeiting equipment in this house."

Everyone was handcuffed for safety purposes and special agent Ryle ordered his men to search the house. Meanwhile Jacob told agent Ryle he would look at the barn area.

Jacob first looked around the building itself and could not detect anything unusual such as freshly dug ground. Inside there were five stalls. Three of them had horses. He had seen the pasture at the back where the horses could probably be let out to roam around and munch on fresh grass. He let the horses out one by one as the other agents were searching the rest of the barn. The empty stalls appeared to be just that.

There was something about the middle stall, where a beautiful black stallion had been, that appeared to be different. He couldn't figure it until he stepped out of the stall and backed away from it. Now he had a full front view of the three stalls where the horses had been kept. After staring straight-ahead for a couple of minutes he let out, "That's it!" so loud that two agents came rushing to his side.

Jacob said to the two men, "Do you see anything unusual about those three stalls in front of us?" he asked.

They both stared, looked and said, "No, Mr. Schreiber, they look like stalls for horses. We can't see anything different."

Jacob said, "Look carefully at the center one. Now do you see that it is shorter in depth than the other two?"

The two men looked in disbelief. "You're right, sir, it appears now that the center stall is not as deep as the other two. The back wall seems to come out a bit," said one of the agents.

Jacob walked into the stall again and went directly to the back wall where he started to touch and push. All of a sudden, two planks caved in. He was able to push more planks out of the way. What appeared to be a mound about four to five feet high was covered with a tarpaulin. Jacob pulled the tarpaulin and there it was in all its glory: a printing press. To the right of it were several boxes stacked cleanly. To the right of the boxes, a stack of what looked like leather pouches. Jacob asked one of the agents to get Special Agent Ryle over here from the main house.

When Don Ryle arrived Jacob said, "We found the jackpot, my friend. Just look at all those boxes. I bet they are full of printed counterfeit money," concluded the gumshoe.

"Wow!" said Ryle. "Let's open the boxes and see what's in there."

The men went at it quickly and sure enough, the boxes contained counterfeit government bills in denominations of $20s, $50s and $100s.

"A couple of you stay here and the rest follow me to the house," Agent Ryle said. When they got to the house, he informed Josh and his band of crooks they were all under arrest for being in the possession of counterfeit government bills. He then asked one of his men to go to the gate and see if the paddy wagons he had ordered had arrived.

Turning to Jacob he said, "Well, my friend, it was worth getting up early. As the old saying goes, 'the early bird gets the worm.' This time we got a whole can of worms." Looking at the handcuffed men, Ryle said, "Which one of you killed Carl Murdoch?" They all stared down and no one spoke.

Two paddy wagons had driven to the front of the house. The men were separated and loaded in the police wagons. The wounded guard had been attended to so that he was no longer bleeding.

The men went back to the gate and brought all the cars up including the pick-up truck needed to load up the printing press.

"Thanks for your help, Jacob. I understand from one of my men that you were the one who discovered the set up. We're going to make a last sweep of the house and gather as much evidence as we can. If we locate something that will be helpful in determining the one who killed Murdoch, you'll be the first to know. If you want to leave now, I'll ride with one of my people. Let's stay in touch. Later I'm going to need a statement from you about your findings in the barn," the special agent concluded.

By the time Jacob got back to his office, it was mid-morning. Anne greeted him with a smile and asked him if he had slept well.

"Yes I did, until three this morning. Then I joined the FBI and we raided The Sons of God's ranch outside of Lancaster at five this morning. We found what we were looking for. A printing press and boxes of counterfeit money ready for dispersal. Here, I was able to sneak some samples out," as he handed his secretary three different bills.

Anne pulled her wallet from her purse and took out a twenty-dollar note to make the comparison with the counterfeit one. "My god, Jacob, this is so similar I can't tell the difference," she said.

Jacob said, "Here let me show you. You see this signature on the one I just handed you. Now look at the signature on the one you took from your purse. You can tell there is a slight difference. However, who would know that in a busy place unless they had a special machine to detect it. In addition, the texture of the paper is not identical to the one from the treasury department." He started to walk towards his desk and suddenly turned around, "Could you come in my office for a moment, please?" said the private eye.

"What I have to say will be very short, to the point and I would appreciate if you didn't question me on it. Is that clear to you?" She nodded her understanding with raised eyebrows. Jacob went on to tell his faithful secretary about the break up with Lorraine and the reasons she had given him. Anne did say she was sorry for him, but did not question him on the subject.

"I have to go to San Pedro again today. Mr. Plant told me he would be getting some containers from customs close to noon," he informed his secretary. "Anne, I tried this last telephone message several times and the line is always busy. Could you try it for me and if it's still busy get the Telephone Company to check on it?" Having said that he called James Plant to let him know he was on his way and would be there before noon.

**CHAPTER EIGHT...**

The last few days had been quite hectic ones for Jacob. The break up with Lorraine was still on his mind. He thought he had built a strong relationship. In his wisdom, he realized that time had not been on his side. Too short of a courtship to make such a serious decision. He thought the next time he would not be in such a hurry. Anne had left him a message about the busy telephone line. She apologized, all her fault for wrongly transposing the last two digits. The secretary further said she called Marlene Bay and apologized to her too.

The woman was waiting for Jacob's call today. He dialed the right number this time and when a woman's voice answered he said, "This is Jacob Schreiber, may I speak to Mrs. Bay, please?"

A voice sounding like someone who has laryngitis said, "This is Marlene Bay, Mr. Schreiber. I was wondering if you could come by to see me. I have a problem I would like you to handle for me. My nephew, Jack Fundalee, recommended that I speak with you about my problem."

"I could come by your house around eleven this morning if it's okay with you," said the gumshoe.

"Good. Let me jot down your address, and as I said I'll see you in about three hours," concluded the private eye.

*So, the District Attorney recommends that his aunt pay for my services instead of the free services from the LAPD.* Jacob thought that maybe Fundalee did not want to appear to be in a conflict of interest situation. *I must have made a good impression on him. First I'll see what the woman wants and if I can be of service to her. I'll just charge her my regular fee. After all* Jacob thought, *I don't want the DA to feel I'm doing him a favor. It would not look good if some nosey reporter ever found out about a private eye being friendly with the DA, and doing him personal favors on the side. I wonder if her husband is part of this big law firm, Jonathan, Murray, Lopez and Bay. They handle just about any legal matter you can think of, including immigration.*

"Good morning boss," Anne said as she handed Jacob a cup of coffee and his favorite doughnut. "Anything exciting happening in your world today?" said a cheerful secretary.

"What did you have in your cereal this morning to be in such a happy mood? Don't get me wrong, I like it when you come in here full of laughs. It makes for a good working day. I reached Mrs. Bay a few minutes ago. Did you know her nephew, the DA, recommended my services to her?" Jacob said.

Anne replied, "I thought you knew that. The Bay family is an old Los Angeles establishment. They have been here forever. I read a biography on the great grandfather, Alastair Graham Bay, who had built a shipyard in Long Beach at the turn of the century. Quite a family history with old money as they say. She must have something special for a private investigator to do, and Mr. District Attorney thinks enough of you to recommend your services."

"I'm glad he did, but my point really is that he has trust in me as an individual and private investigator. He knows I'll go straight to the facts. Some private eyes like to embellish the situations. I don't, as you know. Our type of work is like any other business except that our product is investigating. You have taken special courses at the college level where a person is exposed to law enforcement agencies and their roles. You've also taken studies about the criminal mind and how one should deal when confronted with such a person. Your knowledge of the world of investigation goes beyond what the average gumshoe on the street knows. This is why I pay you double what a regular secretary would cost me. You are a valuable component of my organization and soon, because I have it in mind and if your husband agrees to it, I am going to ask you to be my partner in business." Jacob couldn't help but see the raised eyebrows. "No need to be surprised, Anne. I think that when you finish your next session of law studies, you'll be ready for what I just said."

"I didn't know you wanted to have me as a business partner, Jacob," said a smiley secretary. "I know business is increasing and much of the small stuff I could handle now. Why me and not a male partner?" Anne asked.

Jacob said, "First of all, Anne, I have complete confidence in your abilities and trust your judgment fully. I know a couple of young men who are going through the police academy training at the present who would be perfect partners. Again, that's three to four years down the road before I would have total confidence in their work. Last and most importantly to me, you are the most qualified person, after me that is, and you deserve the opportunity."

Anne just stood there not knowing what to say to this man. He was like a big brother to her and she trusted him fully. Convincing her husband when the time came, would most likely be a major endeavor. As she turned to go to her desk the telephone rang. "Schreiber Investigation, how can I help you?" she said. "Just a moment, Lieutenant, he's right here."

"Good morning, Mr. Jones, how can I be of service to you today?" Jacob said with a jesting tone in his voice.

"First of all, Jacob, you could invite me for a cup of coffee since I'm no more than a city block away from your office. Good, this time the coffee is on me.

I do need to talk business with you, if you have time. See you in ten minutes, my friend," concluded the head of LAPD's homicide.

The telephone rang again and this time Anne kept talking with the person, writing down information and asking questions. Jacob knew how valuable Anne was to the business. Understanding the principles of civil law as well as criminal law was crucial to a good investigator.

"Jacob, I think you are going to like taking this client on board. I hope you do. His name is Carlos Knibble and happens to be the new union Chief for the Actors' Guild. He wants to sue his wife for divorce because he knows, at least this is what he said to me, she's sleeping around with a young actor by the name of Ricardo Alvarez. Alicia Bell-Knibble is very rich. She inherited stocks from her father and owns four big commercial buildings in downtown Los Angeles. You remember Alvarez, he played a lead role in those cowboy movies that have a Mexican flavor," Anne concluded.

"Give me the telephone number, I'll call him before Lieutenant Jones gets here with our coffees." The telephone rang four to five times before a male voice answered. "This is Jacob Schreiber, may I speak with Carlos Knibble, please?"

"Thank you, Mr. Schreiber, this is Carlos. As I explained to the lady, I need to talk with you. May I come to see you this afternoon? Yes, three o'clock is fine."

Jacob thought business was growing fast. Two new possible clients in less than two hours. He did need a partner. His thoughts were going back to the Carl Murdoch murder when Bill Jones came in with coffee and doughnuts.

Jacob looked at the doughnuts and put his hand in his pocket bringing out a handful of change. "Anne, how much of a tip should I give the delivery-man?" he said with a laugh in his voice. Bill Jones smiled and sat down across from Jacob.

"You are always getting the coffee, so this time I thought I'd return the favor," Bill Jones said. "I have some new developments regarding The Red Dahlia, but not in reference to the murder of Carl Murdoch as yet. The information Special Agent Ryle was able to gather in Lancaster is taking us in several directions. There is a contact man who apparently hangs around the West LA bar. We don't know his name yet. What we know has to do with stolen goods like jewelry, paintings and antique heirlooms from estates in the affluent and older areas of Los Angeles and Orange Counties. So far, what I understand about the sale and distribution of these stolen goods is being handled partly by this contact person out of The Red Dahlia. One of our informers has also told us there is a prominent individual behind the scene. Who that person is yet, we don't know. I figured if we coordinate our efforts—yes, I mean yours and ours—we should be able to solve the puzzle. You haven't taken a bite from your doughnut yet, Jacob. You seem to have your mind elsewhere. Did you understand everything I've just said?" concluded the homicide detective.

"I heard you loud and clear Lieutenant. I'm just thinking about Carl Murdoch's elimination. He knew a hell of a lot more than what he wrote down on paper. I know you're pursuing the murder side of things, but all these side occurrences are somehow interconnected, don't you think?" Jacob said.

"I agree with you, Jacob. I have involved my colleagues from Fraud and other departments, but have retained the coordination since the prime crime here is murder. Our FBI friend told me some high profile lawyer has come forward to act on behalf of Josh and his Sons of God. Ryle also said none of them had any Ids with them, not even a driver's license for the bus and two pickup trucks found at the group's compound. The registrations are from out of state, Utah ,I believe. The FBI is checking on that now. They all denied any knowledge or having anything to do with the counterfeit money seized in the barn. I understand you were the one who found the secret cache. Tell me, how did you do it, Jacob?" concluded the Lieutenant.

"It was not that difficult, Lieutenant. First, I let the horses out to pasture. If I had not done so, I don't think we would have ever found the phony bills. You see, once the horses were out of the way it was easy to inspect the stalls. Something kept bothering me as I walked through the middle stall. I decided to back away and look from twenty to thirty feet out. Then I saw it. The middle stall was not as deep as the other two. The back wall seemed to bulge forward, not very much, but if you kept your eyes on it, you noticed a slight difference. This gave me the idea there could be a false wall at the back of the stall. Of course, having a beautiful black stallion in there distracted from what they had done. Clever they were, and I just got lucky I guess. The young FBI officers would have never thought of moving the horses. In fact, they looked as if they were afraid of horses. I wasn't. When I was a little boy, my grandfather had a farm where he raised horses. I had my favorite one, his name was Prince and that he was. Every Sunday my father would take my mother and me to visit and I had a chance to ride Prince. You see, Lieutenant, things that you do in your youth always come to the surface at one time or other. Thanks for the coffee, next time it will have to be on me," Jacob said.

The Lieutenant said, "You certainly are not Irish, Jacob, but somehow you have the luck of the Irish sticking to you. I would like to take a second look at the personnel from The Red Dahlia, but since they know I'm with the LAPD some may not want to talk with me. My purpose of coming here this morning was really to ask you a favor. Would you mind, when you have the time, finding out all the information one can possibly find on these people. Someone in there must know more than what has been said so far. My feeling is that you may get lucky and find who did Carl Murdoch in. You have a puzzled look on your face, Jacob. Do I take that as a no?" the Lieutenant concluded.

"Not at all Bill, your comments just brought some other thoughts to the surface. I had intended to go back to The Red Dahlia anyway. I'll let you know what I find my friend," Jacob said.

**CHAPTER NINE...**

Marlene Bay was standing at the entrance of the living room when Jacob came to call on her. A woman in her mid-sixties she stood tall and straight with long, flowing salt and pepper hair. To the private eye, this elegant woman appeared to be growing old gracefully. "Would you like some tea, Mr. Schreiber?" the lady asked.

"That would be very nice, Mrs. Bay. You have some wonderful paintings on your walls. Did you acquire them yourself?" Jacob asked to break the ice and warm up the conversation. "I see that you have a good eye for some of Gauguin's early work."

"I didn't know a private detective could also be an art lover. Did you go to art school, Mr. Schreiber?" Marlene Bay asked.

Jacob noted a bit of snobbism in her tone but chose to ignore it. "Painters always fascinated me. I read many biographies and visited several museums across North America. That's how I acquired my knowledge, Madam." Jacob took a seat where Mrs. Bay had motioned him. "I have been wondering why you would not use the services offered through the

DA's office. Any particular reason for you to want a private investigator, Mrs. Bay?"

"Yes, there is, Mr. Schreiber. What I want you to do is to find out what one of my employees is mixed up in. I own several businesses in the greater Los Angeles area. I have a jewelry shop in Beverly Hills, a men's clothing store in the Wilshire district, three major restaurants and two night clubs including The Red Dahlia in West Los Angeles. Now you can see where I could place my nephew in a conflict of interest should his department be involved investigating my private affairs," Marlene Bay concluded.

Jacob said, "I will need the name or names of the people you want me to check on. I will also need to know a bit of information on their background, if you have it, that is. Anything I find that is not related to the murder of Carl Murdoch, I will relate to you. Anything else will have to go through the LAPD Homicide division under Lieutenant Jones. Are we clear on that before I begin?" the gumshoe said.

"I have no objection, Mr. Schreiber. All I want to do is find out about my employees and what they are up to. I cannot have my family name involved in murders, drugs and god knows what else they do in nightclubs. I have a check here for a retainer. I'll pay you in full once you complete your investigation. Is that the normal way you do things?" Mrs. Bay asked.

Jacob said, "It's the only way I do business, Mrs. Bay. Now, if you provide me with the information on your personnel, I'll be ready to get to work. May I ask you how long you have been the owner of The Red Dahlia and is the ownership in your name alone?" the private eye questioned.

Mrs. Bay said, "It's under a holding company which belongs to my husband and me. You know my husband William Alexander Bay, don't' you? He's a retired judge who is also a partner in a Corporate Law Firm downtown. I control the holding company and I am listed as the president and CEO."

On his return to the office Jacob couldn't help but think how some wealthy people are totally unaware of what the real world is about. Her nephew must have told this lady about the murder in one of her privately owned establishments. She must know about the type of people who frequent bars such as The Red Dahlia. Once his investigation is over, he thought he might want to suggest for her to sell the nightclub to keep her family name out of public scandals.

Instead of driving straight to the office, he decided to go directly to The Red Dahlia. Now that The Sons of God were out of the way, other staff might feel safer giving information they were somewhat reluctant to speak about before. The murder of Chuck Long, the second murder in or around the same place in less than three weeks, would make it somewhat difficult for Jacob to question anyone.

As the gumshoe walked into the bar, he noticed there were not as many patrons as the times before. The murders must have kept the clients away. He noticed a new face behind the bar and walked right up to him. "Hi! My name is Jacob Schreiber, are you the new barman?"

"No," replied the man. "I'm Sol, the manager. Just had to fill in until I can find a good reliable bartender. You look like a guy who could do this job, are you interested? It pays well," said the manager.

Jacob said, "Not really looking for work, but I was looking for you if you happen to be Sol Leitman. I'm a private investigator looking into the murders of your former bartender and Carl Murdoch's too. Where were you when these killings occurred?" Jacob asked.

"I happened to be on vacation in Hawaii when Murdoch was killed, but was home when Chuck Long was done in. I don't think I could give you anymore than what you heard from Chuck the night you talked to him. The police already asked me all the questions I'm going to answer," said an aggravated bartender. "Do you want a drink, or are you here strictly to talk? What did you say your name was? Schreiber? That's right, you're Jacob Schreiber, a private eye sniffing around for something." Sol walked away to serve a client at the other end of the bar.

Jacob noticed the man who had just walked in looked somewhat familiar to him. He also noticed that this man and the bartender were whispering to each other and looking in his direction. *If only I could remember who this guy is,* Jacob thought. *Well there's only one way to find out,* he muttered to himself as he got up and walked to the end of the bar. "I couldn't help but wonder, where have I have seen this face before! Do I know you from somewhere?" Jacob asked.

"Bug-off, gumshoe, before I flatten you right here," the man said.

"That's easier said than done mister, but you're welcome to try," Jacob shot back keeping his eyes on the creep.

The guy quickly turned around and tried to side punch Jacob without success. The gumshoe grabbed his arm, in one motion flipped him on his back, and held his right shoe against the man's face.

"I told you it was easier said than done. What did you say your name was?" as he applied pressure to the man's arm forcing him to swear at him. "It is not very nice to use foul language in a public place mister. Now, either you cooperate with me or I shall indiscriminately walk all over that ugly face of yours. What will it be? The choice is yours," Jacob said.

"Okay, okay" the man said. "Let my arm go and I'll talk to you." He got up after Jacob made sure he was not carrying a gun, and sat at the bar. "What is it you want from me, gumshoe?"

"Let's begin by who you are with an ID to prove it," Jacob said.

The man pulled his wallet out of his back pocket, retrieved his driver's license and handed it to Jacob. It showed him to be Antonio Candellara. Then Jacob remembered where he had seen him before. "Now, I remember who you are. One of Tony Padilla's former gofers, weren't you?" Jacob said. "Did you switch over to the other slime ball, what's his name, Profacini?" Jacob said. He waited a few seconds for the answer to come forward.

Candellara said, "Vito's going to get you for this, Mr. Private Eye. You're getting too big for those shoes of yours. Maybe we'll outfit you with good solid cement ones before dropping you in the ocean."

"You can tell your friend Vito that I am ready for him anytime he wants to meet with me alone. Of course that will be impossible because he's as big a coward as you are."

Jacob reached for the telephone the bartender had placed in front of the Mafioso, and dialed Bill Jones' private number. He got an answer before the first ring finished. "Hey, my friend, why don't you come meet me at The Red Dahlia. I may have a present here for you. Yes, it's urgent. You're just around the corner, good we'll wait for you," Jacob concluded.

"Who the hell was that?" Tony Candellara asked. "I'm not sitting here waiting for anybody," as he made a move to get up. Jacob pushed him back on the stool vigorously. "I wouldn't try to go away if I were you. It's not polite to walk away from the LAPD's head of homicide who has many questions to ask and hopefully get answers from you to save your ass from going to jail for a long long time."

As he finished his words, Jacob saw Lieutenant Jones and an associate walk into the bar. During all that time, Sol the bartender, had stayed away from Jacob. Now with the police inside, he didn't dare come over to find out what was going on.

"What have we got here, Jacob?" the Lieutenant asked.

"I think this guy—by the way his name is Tony Candellara—knows something about the murder of Chuck Long. He might also know about Carl Murdoch's too." Jacob got closer to the Lieutenant and whispered in his ear that a search of the man's pockets may give him a reason to book him.

Lieutenant Jones ordered the man to stand up and place his hands on the edge of the bar where he could see them and at the same time spread his feet apart. "What have we got here?" as the Lieutenant pulled several small packets from different pockets of Candellara's jacket. He turned to his associate and told him to call a squad car as he was handcuffing the gangster.

Jacob said, "I forgot to tell you, Lieutenant, that you will be sorry for doing what you are doing to this man. He happens to be one of Vito's gofers, who will obviously send a good mouthpiece to get him out on bail, unless he's a strong suspect in a murder or two. He gave me the whole low-down about cement shoes and all that. Real nice person this Tony is. Don't be too rough on him," the gumshoe concluded in a sarcastic tone. Again, he whispered to the Lieutenant to leave the bartender to him for another day.

As they were finishing their talk, the squad car arrived and took the gangster to jail. Bill Jones and Jacob had a small private talk and the homicide detective left the premises. Jacob went back to the stool he had previously occupied and motioned the bartender to come over. "Do you think you and I could now have a private talk together, or would you prefer I come over to your residence later?" Jacob asked with a smile on his face.

"My shift ends in fifteen minutes. If you can wait 'till then, it would make it much easier for me. Is this okay with you, Mr. Schreiber?"

Jacob noticed the change in the man's tone and said it would be fine. He ordered a beer and walked to a booth away from the other customers to wait. Some twenty minutes later Sol came to join him with a beer in hand.

The manager-bartender said, "I must tell you, Mr. Schreiber, that I am not very comfortable talking or being seen with you. Chuck's departure from this world was partly due to his being seen and overheard talking with you."

Jacob answered, "No need for you to worry, Sol. If you take a look, you will see that not even one of Profacini's goons is around. Besides, you saw how I can handle the best of them," he concluded with a tone of sarcasm in his voice.

"I don't know what you want but I'm scared of those guys. They came in here some six months ago and made me an offer I couldn't refuse. Either I paid for protection or they would first break my legs, then my arms and so on, until I agreed to their demands. They mean business, you know. Okay, let's get on with what you want to know," Sol reluctantly said.

"Let's begin with the murder of Carl Murdoch and then you can tell me about Chuck Long. I would also like to find out what you know about Josh and his Sons of God clan," the private eye said.

Guy Beaulieu

## CHAPTER TEN...

For Jacob, the morning walk to the office had
been quite eventful. First, there were three ambu-
lances picking up people that appeared to have
overdosed. Then, some drunken punk had thrown a
brick through the plate glass window of a Hollywood
Boulevard jewelry store. Two blocks further, four
LAPD officers were holding three men at gunpoint
and had them laying face down on the pavement.
Most people did not even pay attention to the go-
ings-on. Everyone was in a hurry to get to work.
Since the war was over the suppliers of military
needs had to lay off thousands of workers. Many had
left the Southern California area, but those that
stayed behind were struggling to survive. The crime
scene was on the rise. The demand for security was
increasing week by week.

Even Jacob's own private eye business had more
than doubled. What he used to handle alone, like
photography, he now hired experts in a specific field
to help him cope with the increased demand. All
these thoughts were going through his mind as he
reached his office building. As usual he ran up the
stairs two at a time. He walked into the office, quick-

ly checked if Anne had left him any messages. When he saw there were none, he went back downstairs to his favorite coffee shop for his morning jolt of caffeine and doughnut.

No sooner was he back in the office that he heard the front door open. He took a peek and to his astonishment saw Mrs. Marlene Bay walking in. "Good morning Mrs. Bay, what brings you to my part of the world?" Jacob said.

Mrs. Bay said, "I got a telephone call last night from Sol Leitman who manages The Red Dahlia. He told me he did not appreciate being pushed around by an insignificant private eye. I informed him that as of that moment he was no longer in my employ. Now I need someone to get my keys from him and have the locks changed. I couldn't think of anyone else but you who could do this effectively. I'll pay for it. It's just that I have to find me another person immediately. Would you be able to give me that service today, Mr. Schreiber?" Marlene Bay concluded.

"It's not something I would normally do, Mrs. Bay, but under the circumstances I'll gladly do it. Do you want me to handle the changes for the locks or do you already have someone in mind?" Jacob asked.

"I'll leave it all up to you, Mr. Schreiber. My new manager should be there by eleven o'clock this morning. His name is Rodney Spikes. He's thirty-two years old, tall and blond. Athletic type young man.

He's a friend of my nephew's family. Have you deposited the check I gave you the other day? If not, I would like to replace it with this more generous one," said Marlene Bay. "By the way my husband has heard good talk about you from some of his colleagues. I already knew that from my nephew, but thought you should know it too, Jacob. Would you mind much if I called you Jacob?"

"Thank you for the good words, and yes, please call me Jacob. Otherwise, I'll feel too old. Let me check my safe for a moment, maybe my secretary did not make any deposit in the last couple of days. Here it is, Mrs. Bay, the check you gave me for $5,000," as he handed it to her. She in return gave him the new check.

Jacob quickly glanced at it and saw it was for $8,500. He did not say anything about the amount. "I'll make the arrangements to change the locks this morning. I would imagine the day bartender would be there by ten. Am I correct in my assumption?" Jacob asked.

"You are, Jacob, and please let me know once you have the locks changed. Have the man make four sets of keys. Three sets you'll give to Rodney and the fourth one is for me. You can bring it over whenever you have a chance to do so. I must go now, my chauffeur is waiting downstairs. Thank you again for being so flexible."

Jacob thought about Sol who had not been happy with his visit at the bar the other day. He didn't know Mrs. Bay had hired Jacob or he would not have complained to her. The gumshoe noticed the constant nervousness on Leitman. He must have been skimming some money from the top. Being afraid of Profacini was not necessary. All he had to do was tell the owner about it and she would have informed her nephew the DA. He, in turn, would have taken care of the problem. As his thoughts were racing through his mind, Anne walked in.

"Good morning, Jacob. You're early today, anything special going on?" she asked.

"There is, my dear secretary. Here's a check from Mrs. Bay to replace the one I took out of the safe and returned to her. She decided to up her retainer and gave me an unusual assignment I promised to fulfill. Would you call the guy we always use for changing locks and have him meet me at The Red Dahlia in West LA around ten this morning. Next, see if you can find Lieutenant Jones for me. I'll go downstairs and get us a fresh coffee," Jacob said as he walked towards the main office door.

When he returned to his desk, Lieutenant Jones was on the telephone. "Good morning to you my friend," Jacob said. "I just want to make sure you and I get together for lunch today. I will have some interesting information for you. Are you available and if so, where would you like to meet. Sounds good to me Lieutenant, see you at Hollywood Park around half past twelve," the private eye concluded.

Jacob made a few telephone calls including one to the DA's office where he spoke with Jack Fundalee to first thank him for the recommendation to his aunt Marlene Bay. He also suggested that she might be better off selling the investment she had in The Red Dahlia. Owning a nightclub where drug dealings and murders occurred too often was not good for the reputation of a retired judge. The DA told him he would consider his comments on his next visit with Aunt Marlene.

When Jacob arrived at The Red Dahlia, the lock and key man was waiting for him. He proceeded to change the locks on all doors. He was done within an hour and handed the private detective the keys he had requested.

"You must be Rodney Spikes," as a young man walked in the bar. "I'm Jacob Schreiber. Mrs. Bay had asked me to have the locks changed. I did, and here are three sets of keys for you." Jacob also informed him that Sol Leitman had given him all the keys he had in his possession, including the ones for the locks on the bar doors etc., as he handed them to him. The gumshoe left the building satisfied the new manager would not need him for the time being.

When he arrived at the Hollywood Park restaurant, Bill Jones was already seated at a corner table reading the day's newspaper. "Well, Mr. Detective, you beat me to the draw today. Can I offer you a drink before lunch? The look on your face tells me you are wondering why. No reason, just that I'm going to have one myself and I hate to drink alone," Jacob said.

The Lieutenant said, "If you insist, I'll have a cold beer. It has been hot lately and driving around does not make it cooler. So you told me you may have some interesting information. I hope it concerns The Red Dahlia," Bill Jones said.

Jacob said, "I had an interesting two days. It all began at the bar in question when I called and you arrested Tony Candellara. Some thirty minutes after you left, Sol Leitman who was the manager, and who no longer works there, told me some interesting facts we both forgot to look into. The regular trio of Tim Huckles, Jim Bates and David Storm who play jazz four nights a week were not questioned as much as other staff members were. He, Sol, wondered why. Especially when musicians are known to be more inclined to use drugs than ordinary people are. He also said that the leader of The Sons of God, whom we know as Josh, is not his real name. In fact, he said, he's an ex-convict who had done a five-year term for counterfeiting and other good things such as armed robbery. Sol mentioned he wouldn't be surprised if this Josh character was not also a hitman for the mob. He avoided him as much as possible, fearing they would ask him to be involved in their phony bill scheme. Sol was afraid of Vito Profacini whom he met once when he came to visit and listen to jazz music. From all this information, I assumed the former manager never told Candellara or his boss the bar was owned by a relative of the DA himself. I did some checking on the three musicians and could not find anything unusual in their past. I do have their social security numbers and I thought maybe you could make a criminal check to see what comes up. That's about it so far, Lieutenant," Jacob concluded.

The homicide detective said, "You are right when you say we neglected the three musicians. I'll have to look into their past activities a little better this time around. I don't know these three men. Do you by any chance have any information on them?" the Lieutenant asked.

"I certainly do," Jacob said. "Come by the office later and I'll give you a personnel file I have on each one. Marlene Bay had asked me to check the background of all the staff from The Red Dahlia. She's upset about the bad publicity her place got and hired me to dig where the LAPD usually can't go. You probably don't know she's the DA's aunt, and did not want to place him in a conflict of any kind. That's why I'm there," the gumshoe concluded.

On his way to the office, Jacob noticed a black car following him. He made several turns just to confirm the fact, and, yes, the car was following every move he made. A few streets further he succeeded in letting the black car pass by him and took note of the license plate number. At the same time, he saw the two men sitting in the front looking all over, to see where he had disappeared. He had no doubt they were from the Profacini stable. Again they were using scare tactics, which would work on the public, but Jacob Schreiber was not easy to scare day or night. He made sure his .45 special was with him and ready for use, if it became necessary. Jacob was just about to pull away from the curb when he noticed a black Cadillac coming towards him at a speed faster than one would normally travel at on city streets. He barely had time to duck as bullets when flying by over his head. The car was too far for him to have had the opportunity to catch the plate number. His encounter with Candellara was the cause of this, he had no doubt. He rushed to his parking lot behind the office building.

From his desk, he dialed the Lieutenant's private line. After the third ring Bill Jones answered. "Homicide, Jones here."

"This is Jacob, Lieutenant. I believe the Profacini boys are at it again. As I left the parking lot of the Hollywood Park, I noticed a black car tailing me. I succeeded in losing him. Then, as I was just ready to leave the curb I heard the roar of an engine and just had time to duck avoiding a visit to the morgue. I was lucky on the first one and got a license number. Could you check it out for me and then I'll decide on what to do with the information. I know what you're thinking, Lieutenant, but I didn't see who shot at me. I'm just guessing it has to be someone associated with Vito Profacini since I ruffed up one of theirs and had him booked."

"I don't doubt it either, Jacob, but this time let me handle it my way if you don't mind. We can't have open warfare on the streets of the City of Angels, can we now? I will let you know whom the car is registered to, but give me a day to look into it, then you do your thing. I would also ask you to be extra careful for a while. Is that fair enough, my friend?" the Lieutenant concluded.

**CHAPTER ELEVEN...**

Rodney Spikes was told to be on the lookout for protection demands from the Profacini boys. If this did happen, he was to notify the DA's office right away. Chances were it would happen. In any event, Spikes was not a rookie at running a nightclub and The Red Dahlia was no different.

Jacob had planned an organized surveillance of Jeff Plant's warehouse facilities in San Pedro. Don Ryle had agreed to have two of his agents go along with him. They were to do some undercover work to see if they could flush out whoever was stealing from the containers. Drugs would certainly become part of this operation, along with some other surprises. Being a snoop can sometimes place the individual doing the snooping in a very precarious position. Case in hand when one of the agents sent with Jacob noticed smoke coming from holes drilled in a large container. He immediately informed Jacob and the other agent. They went to the container, noticed it did not have a seal or lock on it. When they opened the doors, to their surprise they found fifteen to twenty Chinese men and woman huddling in a corner of the container, scared to death. The smell was unbearable and all appeared to be cold and hungry. Jacob rushed to Plant's office and got him to call the FBI, customs and the Port authorities to handle the situation. The whole scene became a distraction to the actual reason they were there in the first place. Smuggling people into the USA was nothing new. It had been going on for a long time. Usually the smuggled people in this part of the country came from south of the border in Mexico. The private eye had to explain to Jeff Plant his reason for being there with FBI agents out of Los Angeles. They didn't let this incident distract them too long. Jacob and his two 'assistants' went back inside the warehouse and positioned themselves in different areas where they could see each other and keep an eye on the goods at hand.

An hour went by without anyone coming in or out close to the containers. Maybe the arrival of customs officers, FBI agents and others from the Sheriff's department scared the thieves off. Jacob was about to call the whole thing off when he heard some noise coming from behind him. He crouched so as not to be seen. At the same time, he motioned to the two agents so they would be aware of what was going on. From the bills of lading, Jacob already knew the contents of the six remaining containers. They were all scheduled for delivery in the next couple of days. Then he saw them. Three men dressed like dockworkers so as not to be noticed. They went directly to the smaller of the remaining containers. The inscription on the side said: 'Olivetti Oil Company, Palermo Italy.' The tall one in the front pulled a key out of his pockets and unlocked the three locks, which were holding the door closed.

While all this was going on, Jacob was keeping an eye on the three men getting access to the container. Then he saw a fourth man backing a pickup truck right to where the other three were standing. Within minutes, they started to load long boxes, six in total, then some smaller boxes, which they stacked on top. They were just about ready to leave when Jacob gave the signal to the FBI agents who came out of hiding guns in hand. The four men were startled. One made a move with his hand reaching inside his shirt. Jacob did not hesitate and fired his .45 at the man's shoulder who, while dropping to the ground, also dropped the gun he had been reaching for. The distraction which lasted a few seconds was long enough for the driver to jump back in the truck and start to drive away. Again, Jacob did not hesitate and successfully shot the two rear tires and then the back window of the truck's cab. It stopped and the driver came out with his hands up. The commotion had drawn some of the customs agents from the adjacent warehouse to see what was going on. One of the FBI agents who had come down to San Pedro with Jacob told everyone to freeze and informed them they were under arrest. The four men involved in getting the wooden boxes from the container were immediately handcuffed. The Sheriff's department was called in and took three of them away. The fourth one was taken to the hospital to be patched up.

The FBI, Jacob and three custom agents walked over to the pick-up truck to check on what was being taken away. In the small boxes, they discovered packages after packages of what appeared to be cocaine. The larger boxes contained military rifles and handguns stolen from some base on the East Coast. The remainder of the container from Italy would now have to be checked by Customs and FBI agents.

When Jacob returned to his office, he completed his report on the San Pedro warehouse and had Anne send a copy to Jeff Plant. Now that the thieves had been found and arrested, he could close his file. Next would be an easier job in tailing Olivia Bell-Knibble and her lover Ricardo Alvarez.

The private eye had some good contacts amongst the Hollywood film people. He used one of them to save himself time and get all the personal information he needed on Alvarez. On divorce cases, Jacob never knew how long it would take to find valuable information for his client or how soon he could put an end to the investigation. With a bit of luck and because neighbors always like to gossip, he always found enough material to help his client when court time arrived. This case was no different. Neighbors of Ricardo Alvarez were eager to let Jacob know who was coming in and out of his residence. With notebook and pencil in hand, he was always mistaken for a reporter. He hired his regular photographer to get snapshots of the people traffic in and out of the actor's home. When he returned to the office he gave all of the information to Anne and told her the photographer would have some pictures for the file shortly.

"You have a call from Don Ryle, and it sounded urgent," Anne said.

Jacob went to his office and called the FBI man. "Well, Mr. Ryle, this sounds like valuable information and findings," the private eye said. "There had to be more than just the thefts of small items from the San Pedro warehouse. Now that one Mafia group is incarcerated, the other group has revived the arms connections with Middle Eastern and African countries. You are going to need more than a handful of weapons to make it stick in Federal court. What is most intriguing about this one, is that they haven't stolen the weapons from our military bases here but from resources in Italy, Australia and England," Jacob concluded.

Ryle said, "Thanks to your previous findings, we have a list of people who purchase these weapons. We are going to *liaise* with several international agencies and see if we can either slow the flow or put a complete stop to it. Nothing is easy but now we know how the weapons are transferred. Breaking that up will effectively slow the process, but they'll find another innovative way to smuggle weapons again. Customs and immigration are handling the matter of the Chinese refugees. These people were lucky to be found alive. By the way, one of them spoke English well enough to tell their side of the story. Are you free for lunch tomorrow?" the FBI special agent asked.

"I'll make time for it," Jacob said. "It's important that we meet on neutral ground once a week. This way, we can inform each other about our mutual interests. So, tomorrow at the Brown Derby," the gumshoe said as he put the telephone down.

Jacob was pleased about his relationships with the FBI and the local police. In many instances, it made it easier for him to move an investigation forward. He knew of other private investigators that were not on friendly terms with the LAPD, and they had a hard time getting information from State agencies.

Lieutenant Jones had made arrangements for Jacob to come along with him to the county jail where Grant Smith was being held awaiting a decision from the DA's office whether to put him on trial or not. When they arrived at the detention center, both men were taken to a special waiting room normally used for privacy by lawyers and their clients. The room was institutional-like with a metal table, a stool on one end and a bench on either side. There was another small door at the opposite end from where the Lieutenant and Jacob came in. That door opened and Grant Smith and a guard walked in. Smith was escorted to the end of the table and told to sit there. The guard then left the room.

The Lieutenant introduced himself and Jacob. He told Smith the purpose of their visit and said that the private eye would be conducting the interview.

Jacob began the conversation by asking Smith how old he was and if he had any family here in LA. "I understand you hung around a bar in West LA called The Red Dahlia. Did you ever have a conversation with Carl Murdoch?"

Smith answered, "I had many conversations and drinks with Carl, Mr. Schreiber. He was a good man and always willing to help someone. I'm not sure who killed him, but I do think Josh ordered the killing. This phony evangelist was friends with some tough Mafia characters and I'm sure one of them did Carl in."

"And did you see the actual take down the night it happened? Can you remember everyone who was there?" Jacob asked.

"I wasn't there that night, but I heard plenty from some of my clients the following day. From what I understand, the trio was playing that night and Carl was at the piano. Apparently, someone he must have known told him a friend wanted to talk to him at the back entrance. He did not hesitate and immediately went through the back door. My client told me he never came back in to play music. It was funny, my man said, because the regular piano player, Tim Huckles, came into the bar and went directly to the piano like nothing had happened. Of course, no one knew Carl had been murdered at that time."

"Anything else out of the ordinary your client could have told you? Would you mind giving me his name so I can talk to him?" Jacob said.

"You know what, I don't know his name, just always called him 'Peanuts' because he always has a handful and eats them all the time. He's about thirty years old with dark brown hair, wears his watch on his right arm. He usually comes in the bar around seven. He's about 5'7" or 5'8" and wears old army boots. I've seen him many times hang around with Josh and some of his followers. I wouldn't be surprised if he'd joined that group of freaks. 'Peanuts' is a very talkative guy, 'specially if you buy him a beer or two," Smith concluded.

Jacob and the Lieutenant left the detention center after spending close to an hour with Grant Smith. The only concern they had was about Smith's credibility. Was he telling the truth or just making conversation to help his cause? Jacob figured the man was being straightforward. If he wanted to avoid going to trial, he better be. In any event, a short conversation with 'Peanuts' would confirm if Smith had been putting them on or not.

The Lieutenant dropped Jacob in front of his office building. He would let the private eye do the questioning of Smith's client by himself. The presence of a police officer might be too intimidating for the young addict, and he may not talk. Jacob would be better off on his own. He could be trusted to relay any valuable information back.

When he walked into the office, Anne told him George Murdoch had called wanting to know if he had been able to find new information about his brother's murderer. There was also a call from Jeff Plant who wanted to thank him for the good work he had done and, "Would you send him a final invoice?"

"Mr. Murdoch, Jacob Schreiber here. I'm getting closer to finding out exactly what happened to your brother Carl. No need to worry, George, your fee was sufficient. I'll let you know as soon as I have the final news." Jacob understood the man wanted to have his brother's name cleared. He was sure that someone within The Red Dahlia had not told him everything. The gumshoe was determined to pursue his gut instinct.

## CHAPTER TWELVE...

The life of a private eye can be full of surprises, as when totally unexpected one finds himself in a situation he wishes had not happened. On this warm and sunny Friday morning, just as Jacob approached the entrance to his building, he saw a flash reflection in the glass door. Instinct told him to hit the pavement. He did and probably saved his own life. The whole glass door shattered to pieces and as the gumshoe rolled, pulling his .45 out of its holster he was able to blast the rear window of a speeding Cadillac. A second shot from a kneeing position blew the left rear tire, which caused the driver to lose control, and the car flipped over. In one second flat, Jacob was on his feet moving towards the getaway automobile half a block away when a police car came screeching around the corner. The LAPD officers went directly to the car with guns drawn and ordered the two occupants out. One came out limping, the other was dead. The bullet from Jacob's gun had gone through the rear window and got the man square in the middle of the head. Luckily, the sidewalk was free of people at this early hour of the morning, except for a few stragglers who took cover when they heard the gun shots.

The police officers recognized Jacob immediately and one asked, "Are you okay, Mr. Schreiber?" said the young policeman. "We were just around the corner when we heard the gunshots. An ambulance will be here shortly to take this guy away. Your shot got him in the head. One less for the courts to worry about," said the patrol officer with an indifferent tone.

"Thanks, Officer; only my pants and jacket are ruined from hitting the pavement. Otherwise, I'm as good as new. These guys must be from Profacini's stable. No one else drives a Cadillac around here. I'll talk to Lieutenant Jones later, and thanks for being there so fast," the private eye said.

Jacob saw a taxi dropping someone in front of his building and motioned for him to wait. He got in the cab and went home to change his torn clothing while the driver waited to take him back to his office.

When he returned there was quite a commotion in front of the building. Several people were there questioning a police officer on what had happened to smash the plate glass door and window adjacent to it. He succeeded in sneaking by the crowd and ran up the stairs to his office. To his surprise, Anne had arrived and was all smiles when she saw him come in.

"I was just thinking that maybe you had something to do with the broken glass at the entrance. The police officer did not know what happened. Do you by any chance have any idea about the incident?" asked a concerned secretary.

"I'd be lying if I said I didn't know. On the other hand, if I were made of glass you would have to pick up the pieces now. Some punks wanted me out of the way, but they missed, fortunately. One of them was not so lucky, my shot sent him to the Promised Land. Profacini must want me out of the way real bad to send his jockeys after me. Hoodlums, that's what they are, and dangerous ones at that. Just part of a day's work, Anne. Still want to be a private investigator?" Jacob said.

"You seem to forget Jacob, my father is a Highway Patrolman. He has had to use his revolver on several occasions, even had a shootout with bank robbers once. I'm not afraid of the danger that comes with the job, you know. Because I am a woman does not mean I'm weak or fragile. I'm tougher than you think, Mr. Private Eye," Anne concluded, with a grin from ear to ear.

Jacob said, "I believe you, Anne. You cannot go on in life hiding from reality when you know the ones creating the fear are just cowards. I offered you a partnership a little while ago and I hope you decide positively after you complete your law classes. I have no doubt you will make a great investigator." Just as he finished talking the office door opened quickly and an excited LAPD Lieutenant rushed in.

"You have to quit scaring me like this, Jacob," Bill Jones said. "My office notified me about a shootout at your office building with one person dead. They didn't know who it was as the body had not arrived at the morgue yet. I'm glad to see you're still alive, Mr. gumshoe. I suppose the Profacini boys are after you again. I am going to pay a visit to Vito Profacini today. Either he leaves you alone or I'm going to organize a harassment campaign against him and his businesses. I'm sure he wouldn't like to see smaller attendance at his nightclubs. You know, we at the LAPD can work well together when it comes to a common cause," concluded the homicide Lieutenant.

"Thanks for your concern Lieutenant. It warms my heart to know I still have some friends around who care about my wellbeing. I was just about ready to go for my morning indulgence of doughnut and coffee, care to join me?" Jacob said. The two friends left the office and walked down the stairs together. The relationship between these two men had grown over the months of fighting crime alongside one another.

When he returned to the office, Anne had received a stack of photos to be placed in Carlos Knibble's file. She showed Jacob a half dozen pictures that were certainly compromising for Knibble's wife. He told Anne she could handle the closing of the file now that she had the necessary evidence, and complete the final billing.

"I'm going to the Brown Derby to meet Special Agent Ryle for lunch in case you need to reach me, Anne. Then I'm going to have another visit at The Red Dahlia and try to locate a possible witness to Carl Murdoch's murder. Maybe you should start looking or at least think about finding a reliable secretary soon. You said your classes should be over in about two months. That's just about the right time you need to train a new girl. I'll leave the details up to you," Jacob concluded as he prepared to leave the office.

The Brown Derby was full as usual. If you didn't have a reservation, you were out of luck. Most regulars to the place knew that. Lucky for Special Agent Ryle, one of his men informed him about the place. It took Jacob one quick look around to find him. The two men greeted each other in a friendly manner.

Jacob said, "Is this your first time in the heart of actor-land? Look around you and you'll see many familiar faces you have seen either on the big screen or on the cover of some magazine. This place draws all the big stars, their agents and the Hollywood producers together. It's like a club meeting. Once you've been here, whenever you come back you are treated as a regular just like everyone else. I've picked up many clients in this place. People who wanted protection for a short period of time or just wanted to be able to say they had a bodyguard. They paid and well in advance. I always made sure of that because a shining star today can become a falling meteor tomorrow. This is a bit different to what you were accustomed to in New York and downtown Manhattan. Trust me, Ryle, whether it's on the East Coast or here, crooks are crooks. I do have some information you may want, but let's eat first," the private eye concluded.

The FBI agent said, "What kind of new information do you have for me Jacob? We haven't been able to make any of the Lancaster guys talk about the killing of Carl Murdoch. What we were able to find though, is the real identity of this Josh fellow. He's really an ex-con by the name of Joey Durango, a convicted felon with a specialization in counterfeit money. His file also contained several arrests for violence and investigations into different murders from New York to San Diego by way of Florida. The only conviction was on the bogy bills. This time he's looking at twenty to life term if found guilty. You have a surprised look on your face, did I say something wrong?" the FBI man asked.

"You certainly did not, Don. I was about to inform you that Josh was not who he said he was, but you're a mile ahead of me. One thing you could do that may help both of us is to check your national files for these three names," as Jacob handed Ryle a piece of paper with the names of Tim Huckles, Jim Bates and David Storm. "These are the three musicians who play regularly at The Red Dahlia. I could not find anything locally or statewide on them. They may not be on your list, but who knows what they were up to the last five years. There is one more witness to the Murdoch case I'm trying to find. Should I get lucky, he may have some information on both the drug movements and the phony bill distribution set up. I'm told this man could be a possible key witness for you. May I suggest that you ask one of the two men, who accompanied me in San Pedro to hang around The Red Dahlia, say from four p.m. today. He must not approach me until I signal him, otherwise I may lose my contact."

"This all sounds good to me, Jacob. I'll make sure one of the two or maybe both will be there to back you up. Since this is Hollywood, I'm sure they can play the part. Besides, no one knows them. No one in the Vito Profacini family that is. Let's do this again next week. Look forward to hearing from you," the FBI man said.

Both men left in different directions. On his way to the infamous Red Dahlia, Jacob thought how smart a move he had made when he approached the FBI with information they could use several months ago. The relationship was working well, even better than he expected. In the beginning, he thought it would be a one way affair, from him to them. Time had proven him pleasantly wrong.

As he walked into the club in West LA he immediately noticed the two FBI agents sitting in a booth across from the stage where the musicians would later perform. Don Peter Ryle was true to his word and fast about it too.

He sat on an empty stool and ordered a beer. From his viewpoint, he was able to see everyone sitting around as well as people walking in the door. Jacob had consumed his second beer and was debating whether he should leave or stay when the door of the establishment opened and in walked a specimen right out of a comic book. He was just as Grant Smith had described him, grubby looking. The man walked up to the bar, ordered a beer and with his right hand started to search his pocket for money to pay. Jacob immediately called to the barman, "Put his drink on my tab." The young man looked at Jacob and nodded his head in a thank you sort of way.

"I'm Jacob Schreiber," as he extended his hand.

"Thanks for the beer, Jacob, I'm Tom Peaks," he said before swallowing a handful of peanuts. "Do I know you from somewhere? Your face looks familiar but I do not recall your name. You wouldn't happen to have some good stuff with you by any chance? Know what I mean, a good smoke or something of the sort."

"Sorry Tom, I don't smoke or use drugs. I know you do. My friend Grant Smith told me. I may be able to get you some but first let's go sit in the empty booth. I want to talk with you about something you may know," Jacob said.

Jacob ordered another beer for his newly found friend. They sat in a booth just a few feet away from the two FBI agents who never bothered looking their way.

The gumshoe was trying to quickly figure out how to approach the conversation when Tom looked directly at him and said, "I bet you are a cop, Jacob!"

"You have that wrong, Tom, I'm a private investigator," as he showed him his license and at the same time opened his jacket so Peaks could see the .45 just hanging there. "A friend of mine was murdered in the back alley of this joint some weeks ago. Then, after I had a talk with Chuck Long, he was murdered too. Now, so that you know, Josh the leader of The Sons of God, and seven men from his group are in Federal custody charged with counterfeiting. They'll be there for the long haul, if you know what I mean. It's also believed that Josh, whose real name is Joey Durango, was the hitman in both cases. The reason I'm telling you all this, Tom, is because Grant Smith told me I could trust you and that you would be able to fill in the missing pieces in the puzzle."

Tom Peaks said, "I don't know what you are looking for, Jacob, but I do have some information and it will cost you money."

"I'm willing to pay some now and a lot more if your information turns out to be right. I may even have a nice deal for you. Would you rather we go elsewhere to talk? Good let's get in my car.

**CHAPTER THIRTEEN...**

Anne Dombrowski had taken the final exam of her legal courses, *"The Law and the Criminal Mind, Principles to Apply."* She would have to wait a week before knowing if she passed with full honors and received her certificate. The secretary to one of Southern California most successful Private Eyes already carried a license as a private investigator along with a gun permit. Anne was looking forward to become a partner in Jacob Schreiber's Private Investigation firm. He had offered her the possibility as long as her husband did not object. She had spoken to her father about it and he was in full agreement with her decision. In her purse, she carried a pearl handled .25, but most importantly, she also carried a .32 automatic in a small holster behind her back. Jacob knew about it since he had questioned her about wearing a belt most of the time. He had told her it was a good idea because no one would think a woman would carry a gun anywhere else but in her purse. Now, she thought, moving quickly on finding 'the right girl Friday' to take over her duties was top priority. Anne had someone in mind, a former classmate of hers who had to leave the course on short notice because of a serious illness in her family. Just the same, she would place an ad in the local paper to see the talent available. She was just finishing writing the job advertisement request when Jacob walked in.

"Good morning, Anne, you look preoccupied, something wrong?" the private eye questioned as he placed a coffee on her desk.

"No, Jacob, nothing's wrong. I was just preparing an ad for the local paper. You may have forgotten you made me an offer some time back to become a partner in this business. Well, I'm ready. I've taken the last exam of my course, got my father's agreement, had a difficult time to convince my husband, but succeeded, so I'm going to begin a search for a new 'Girl Friday'." She thought for a moment then said, "I do have someone in mind, a former classmate by the name of Laura Brown. She had to leave the course early because her mother was terminally ill. In case she's not available, I'm preparing an ad for the paper."

"That's great news, Anne. You bet I want you as my partner. The workload has increased threefold in the past few months. You've taken many cases from me, and that has been a tremendous help. I just hope your husband is not upset with me. As I said before Anne, I am ready to reorganize our business. If you want to, we can begin mapping out how the workload is going to be divided between the two of us. Mind you, there are some cases where I will want you to work closely with me." Jacob walked to his office to think about making a move from this old building. His lease was due to be renewed in six weeks. The first priority would be to find a new location with adequate space for three private offices and a large reception area. He heard the telephone ring and then Anne's voice telling him Lieutenant Jones was on the line.

"Good morning to you, Lieutenant. Does the homicide division of the LAPD ever sleep?" Jacob jested. "Oh! I see, you would like to have coffee with me now. You sound as if there's something urgent coming up. I'll have a hot cup of java waiting here for you." For an instant, the gumshoe thought his friend sounded somewhat concerned about something. *Well, I'm sure he'll let me know when he gets here.*

Fifteen minutes later the Lieutenant showed up in Jacob's office with a worried look on his face. "What's up, Bill, you do look as if something serious is really bothering you. You're not sick, are you?" Jacob inquired.

"As a matter of fact, Jacob, illness has nothing to do with what I'm going to tell you. First, the bad news from a police view point. My superior informed me late yesterday that I was to stop giving you special privileges and treat you like any other suspect, sorry, I meant citizen. He feels that my relationship with you is not good for the department. Can you believe that? From now on, I am not to use the department's resources to help you in your private investigations. He feels that I am placing the LAPD and myself in a position of mistrust. Somebody got to the Captain. He's been on the force twenty plus years and was always open to his staff having outside contacts. I'll find out who got to him, then you and I will deal with it. Now for the very bad news I got from a reliable informer this morning. According to this person, Vito Profacini has placed a hit on you. There is a ten grand reward to the person who can corral you and bring you to a prearranged meeting place to dispose of your remains. I would imagine this is the unwritten request. You will have to be doubly careful for a while, my friend," concluded the homicide Lieutenant.

Jacob said, "Don't you think it's rather unusual for a police Captain to order one of his Lieutenants not to make contacts outside the police social network? Either the commissioner or the Mayor is putting a lot of pressure on the Captain. I cannot believe that Jacob Schreiber has become a political football to be used at someone's convenience. You can tell your masters that this kind of political hogwash does not go well with me. I do have a couple of aces up my sleeve, which I was keeping for a special moment. I believe the time has come for this gentle private eye to play hardball. Whoever is responsible for being so weak and going along with demands from a scumbag such as Profacini, is going to pay a high price. When you play with fire, you get burned, as the saying goes. Now it's my turn, Lieutenant. You're looking at me as if I'm crazy. Trust me, my friend, I am not. You remember when I first found a stack of papers and some photographs in Louis the snake's briefcase? Names of prominent people involved with prostitutes and bribes given to local politicians. I'm going to have a talk with our Mayor , Lieutenant, and for safekeeping, I'm going to give you a set of photos and list of names I kept out of the Federal investigation at the time. They were not related to Federal crimes nor did they have anything to do with the stolen military weapons. I just had a feeling some of Louis Billings' little secrets would climb to the surface one day," the gumshoe concluded as he got up and went to his wall safe. When he returned he had an envelope full of incriminating material. He handed the envelope to the Lieutenant. "You hang on to this wonderful little package, Bill, and if anything happens to me you can decide what to do with it. They must have scared the Captain with a no-pension dismissal if he did not proceed as ordered. Don't fret my friend, I'll get us all out of this mess no later than today."

"You don't have to do this, Jacob," Bill Jones said. "I was not going to follow the order anyway. Oh! I would pretend I am, but you know there are so many ways to avoid having the finger pointed at you. The Captain did it reluctantly when he called me in. I could feel it in his tone. He wasn't at ease and told me so. The Commissioner and the Mayor are probably both in debt to the mob. Now, this does not speak well of our top civil servants but it's probably true. If you intend to talk to the Mayor , you first let me find out if the order came from him. It would not be wise to go in there without something to back you up. I know without seeing what's in the envelope you're ready for a fight, Jacob. We both must remember that politicians don't fight clean. They are sneaky and can be dangerous when it comes to their personal lives. Let's prepare as a platoon commander would, that way we can avoid the land mines."

"You're talking like your brother Octavio did during the war, Bill. You really think we should plan this, or at least I should," Jacob said. "You may be right on this one, my friend. There's something that's not kosher in the municipal administration," the gumshoe said as he laid out the contents of the envelope on his desk.

The Lieutenant sorted out some photographs and the two of them acted like schoolboys caught looking at girly books. There was enough on the desk to incriminate the whole City Council.

When the DA called to ask Jacob what was going on, the private eye made his decision to expose

the Mayor . He told Fundalee it was a matter of sur-
vival for him and his friends, including the DA himself. "If you want to see evidence that will knock you
off your seat," he said, "come up to my office now."

Jack Fundalee was there in less time than it
takes to drink a hot cup of coffee. "You really made it
sound urgent, Jacob. When the Mayor himself called
me to get over to his office immediately, I didn't
know what to expect. I just could not believe what I
was hearing. The Mayor of Los Angeles asking the
DA to place a private investigator, namely you, on
the blacklist made me wonder about the integrity of
the Mayor 's office. Not to anger him or make him
suspicious about my relationships, I told him I would
follow his order. I knew in my own head there had to
be something wrong somewhere. Let's have it Jacob," said a perturbed District Attorney.

Jacob pointed to the photographs on his desk
and a list of names he was holding on to. "If you pick
any of these pictures you will recognize some of our
most 'elite citizens' Statewide. I am not ready to di-
vulge the source where I got these photos from, but I
can tell you there are more and it probably is still going on. I can imagine from the grin on your face you
don't think the Mayor looks good in his birthday
suit, especially when the two young girls standing
naked with him don't appear to have reached the
age of consent. I don't suppose the Mayor told you
there is a bounty on my head. His good friend Vito

Profacini gave the order last night and someone passed it on to Lieutenant Jones. You may want to question His Honor about it, and I'm sure he'll lie with a straight face," Jacob concluded.

"Wow," said Fundalee. "This is dynamite, Jacob. Where did you get these jewels, may I ask? Oh! Yes, you just said you didn't want to give away your source yet. I'll go along with that, but can I have a copy of these along with the list you're holding in your hand," said a baffled DA. "This looks like the biggest scandal ever to hit the City of Angels."

"You can certainly have these since Lieutenant Jones wanted you to see them firsthand. Should you decide, and I'm not going to tell you how to do your job, to go after the Mayor , there are a few more people involved including a state Senator. Sex has been the downfall of men since the beginning of time. You, as the DA, had better be careful how you approach this crisis. I was not going to use this card yet, but since someone placed a bounty on my head and the Mayor has the audacity to tell my friends not to have a close relationship with me, I'm on the warpath," Jacob said.

The DA said, "I'm certainly going to confront the Mayor with his allegations concerning you, my department and the LAPD. I have the feeling we are going to have a new civic election sooner rather than later. Before I speak to the Mayor , I am going to have a word with Vito Profacini. Should anything nasty happen to you, I'll inform him that he will immediately be arrested and held on suspicion of having committed a criminal act. I wonder what kind of threat was made to Lieutenant Jones's superior. That again is open political interference with the justice system. May I use your telephone please? Need to call my assistant for an urgent meeting. Wow! This is going to rock the foundation of City Hall."

When the DA had left the office, Jacob informed his secretary what all the excitement was about. He warned Anne to be careful and conscious of her immediate surroundings. The Mayor was easy to eliminate but the 'Godfather of Southern California' would be a bit more difficult to ignore. Having said that, he checked his .45 to make sure it was fully loaded and ready for action. Not since leaving the Marines did Jacob feel pressed for action. *If it's a war they want, a war they will get, he thought!*

## CHAPTER FOURTEEN

The car parked at the curb outside his apartment building did not fit the scene. First, it was parked in a manner that would allow the driver a fast getaway. It sometimes pays off to look out the window before hitting the pavement. Jacob knew they were after him. He saw the Mexican gardener mowing the lawn next door. There was also the regular pool-man doing his chores. A plan of action occurred to him. Instead of coming out the front of the building and driving his car, he stopped at the lobby and spoke to the door attendant who also acted as security for the building. James knew Mr. Schreiber well. Following instruction, he opened the front door and motioned to the gardener to come over. He handed the man a $20 after he had agreed to do Jacob's request. It took all but two minutes for the gardener to get in his truck, drive to the corner and stall immediately in front of the Cadillac, blocking its escape route. One of the goons inside the Caddy came out screaming at the Mexican who kept answering as fast as he could in Spanish that his truck wouldn't start. From an observer's point of view, it was hilarious but it gave Jacob enough time to drive away without being shot at or followed. He drove straight to his office laughing all the way.

"Good morning, Anne, anything good going on?" the private eye said with a grin from ear to ear.

"What's so funny, may I ask? Here I sit answering nasty telephone calls on your behalf, and you walk in here as if you just won the World Series. A couple of goons were here looking for you. They left this envelope, which I didn't dare open before you got here. There's a call from Lieutenant Jones, one from Jack Fundalee and one that appears to be a new client, a Mr. Graham Longhaul who said you were referred by Leon Edwards of Texas. So, tell me, what made you laugh so much?" Anne inquired.

Jacob related the earlier incident at his apartment building and they both had a good laugh. He opened the envelope his secretary had given him and frowned as he read the content. He handed the letter over to Anne.

She read aloud,

*'Dear Mr. Schreiber, I want to apologize if any of my employees have been disrespectful towards you. I have informed everyone not to give you any reason to worry. Should you feel that one of my staff was out of line, please let me know immediately and I will make sure it does not happen again in the future. Sincerely, Vito Profacini.'*

"Wow! Jacob, this guy is either bothered by something you're digging into or he wants you to relax in order to catch you off-guard. Now that I think of it, the two goons who came up here were extra polite. So much so, I had my .32 at the ready. I guess Mafiosos like Profacini don't like it when too much attention is being drawn in their direction. I would remain cautious just the same if I were you, Mr. Gumshoe."

"Thanks for the advice, Anne. The DA must have something to do with this. Let's find out what he knows," Jacob said as he walked to his office to make the telephone call. "Good morning to you, Jack. To what do I owe the honor of your call? Oh! I see. Well, ten o'clock is okay with me." Jacob leaned back in his chair trying to guess what the DA would be asking him at this urgent meeting. He did mention Lieutenant Jones. The private eye would feel more comfortable if his friend were there. It must have to do with the photos of the Mayor and Senator he had given Fundalee a few days ago.

When Jacob arrived at the DA's office, he was surprised to see the Mayor sitting next to Lieutenant Jones. His apprehensions did not last long as Jack Fundalee began the meeting right away.

The DA said, "The four of us are here for the sole purpose of reaching what I hope to be a friendly compromise. For the benefit of the Lieutenant and

Mr. Schreiber, I'm asking that you take time to listen to what I propose. First, I want to inform you that when I approached the Mayor with the evidence I had on hand, he did not attempt to deny it. After several hours of talk between the Mayor and myself—by the way I do have a recorded tape of our private conversation—I have agreed to bring the following proposal to both of you. I must say my actions may appear to be contrary to what this office stands for, but on the other hand, I have taken them in the best interest of the people. It would serve no useful purpose to release this evidence to the press or to bring charges against the Mayor. I can see raised eyebrows on you both. This is what the Mayor put forward to me: he will resign for personal reasons immediately if my office can guarantee him that we will not prosecute or leak any of this evidence. That, gentlemen, is what I wanted you to hear in the presence of the Mayor. If you both agree, I'll go along with it and the Mayor will hand his resignation over to the Council this morning. If you need time to think about this, I understand. May I remind you that time is of the essence? We must make a fast decision," the DA concluded.

Jacob said, "Could the Lieutenant and I take ten minutes or so in private before I give you my answer?"

"You certainly may, Jacob, and use my assistant's office, he's away for the day," Fundalee said.

Twenty minutes later Jacob and the Lieutenant returned to the DA's office. "Well, Jack, I must say I'm not too happy with the situation as it stands. The Mayor will certainly not like what he's going to hear from me," Jacob said. "I feel that we are letting a crime slip by right in front of our eyes. The bad part of it is we know who the criminal is and we are not doing a thing about it. On the other hand, it could save the taxpayers of LA a great amount of money if an agreement could be reached. If, before he resigns, the Mayor would agree to apologize to the Captain and the Lieutenant, I would be inclined to go along with the compromise. I've always thought and said; the worst compromise is better than having to go to court." From the corner of his eyes, Jacob could see the Mayor nodding yes in response to his comments. "I would want the Mayor to make his apology now before I leave this room, Jack. I'm sure the Captain will find time to come up if you, as the DA, make the request," Jacob concluded.

There was no doubt the City of Angels would be in better hands if the present Mayor were to announce his retirement from local politics. The state Senator was another ballgame for another time. After the Captain and the Mayor left, Jacob thanked Fundalee for his diplomatic approach to a sensitive situation.

"Now that we can resume our relationship I would like to invite you both to lunch today or tomorrow. Okay? Let's make it tomorrow at the Wilshire Country Club," Jacob said with a smile.

The morning headlines and radio talk shows were filled with the Mayor 's resignation. He declined to give interviews citing a personal situation. The journalistic world was not happy but they would have to live with it. As far as Jacob was concerned, the matter was now a non-issue and would remain that way.

Back in his office, he called Graham Longhaul in Texas. "Jacob Schreiber in Los Angeles, Mr. Longhaul. Anything I can be of help with, may I ask?"

Longhaul said, "I believe you could be, Mr. Schreiber. I own a fleet of one hundred and ten trucks that transport gasoline nation-wide. I also have several railroad cars that do the same with crude oil to different refineries in California, the Midwest and the Pacific Northwest. Recently I've encountered some vandalism on my equipment coming out of Los Angeles. It did not appear to be too serious at first, but when threats to my drivers were made, I just had to do something. Leon Edwards told me about you and assured me you were the best in the business. I'm coming up to Los Angeles tomorrow and would like to meet with you to expand on the comments I just made. Could we possibly get together at the end of the day or better still, let's have dinner if you're available."

"Dinner sounds good, Mr. Longhaul. I'll wait for your call at my office. If you have any tangible evidence concerning the vandalism, would you please bring all you have? This way we'll both have a better handle on it. Look forward to seeing you tomorrow sir," Jacob concluded as he put the telephone down.

Jacob just sat there thinking for a moment. His straightforward approach with people was paying off. Leon Edwards thought enough of his skills to recommend him to someone. He had not planned to do what most private Investigators did; advertise in the local newspapers. Still, referrals kept coming in and business was growing. There was an increasing demand for bodyguards on a short-term basis, as well as home and business security. Changes were happening all around. Since the end of the war, the movie industry was growing and it helped create a number of small businesses with services and equipment needed to bring new movies to the big screen. He was thinking how lucky he was to have a secretary, soon to be a partner, such as Anne when she knocked on his door.

"Come on in," Jacob said in a friendly tone. Anne walked in with a woman roughly her height, size and age.

"Jacob Schreiber, this is Laura Brown who is going to be our new secretary. Laura was with me at the beginning of my courses on the criminal justice system. She left the course at mid-point to look after her terminally ill mother who passed away three weeks ago," Anne said as she introduced Miss Brown.

"Sorry about the loss of your mother, Laura. I'm pleased to finally meet you. Anne has been talking up a storm about you. So you think working for a couple of gumshoes like Anne and me will appeal to you," Jacob said.

Laura Brown said, "Thank you for your kind thoughts about my mother, Mr. Schreiber. I think working for two dedicated people as the two of you are, will be just what the shrink ordered for me. I hope to live up to the standards you have been accustomed to with Anne. I haven't given up on my law enforcement courses yet. For your information, I've enrolled myself for night and weekend classes at UCLA," the new secretary concluded.

"I'm sure you will give us the same professional support we are used to," Jacob said. "Furthermore, should you require any help, Anne or I are always open to talk about things. This is a friendly working office; good or bad, we like things to be out in the open. The work we do on the street is sometimes of a dangerous nature, so being open-minded with each other is important to us. We are going to be moving to larger quarters in a couple of weeks. Your timing to join us is perfect. Welcome aboard, and we'll make sure to initiate you in every aspect of the Investigation business as the weeks go by," Jacob concluded as the two women left his office.

The telephone rang and Jacob answered. "Well, Lieutenant, what's the good news?" Jacob asked.

The Lieutenant said, "Just wanted you to know that the Mayor  issued a press release announcing his retirement from politics for personal reasons. This is the good news for now. Before his stepping down, he again apologized to the Captain and me. He didn't say exactly why he was apologizing but nonetheless, he did. I have another tip on the Carl Murdoch case Let's go to lunch if you have time. There's this bar on Wilshire in Santa Monica that serves prime rib cooked on rock salt. It's one of two things I know the British can do well. The place is either at 18$^{th}$ or 17$^{th}$, it's the only bar around, you can't miss it. Good, see you there, say around half past noon," concluded the homicide detective.

Anne walked into Jacob's office just as he was getting ready to leave for his lunch meeting with the Lieutenant. "So, what did you think of Laura? I think her basic knowledge of what the justice system is about will make her a good secretary. She's better than I am at shorthand and thinks faster on her feet than I do. If you agree, she's ready to start working in two days."

"I'm okay with her. Just make sure she's okay with us and please take care of the office move. I should be back by two or so. Going to lunch with Lieutenant Jones in Santa Monica," Jacob said.

## CHAPTER FIFTEEN

Jacob had awakened in the middle of the night hearing what he thought was the sound of gunfire. From his third floor apartment he had a direct view of the street in front of the building. Parking for the building was underground with a locked gate, which you could only access with a special key. At first, when he looked out of the window he could not see anything out of the ordinary. As he was just turning away from his window, he saw a flash, which had to be the firing of a gun. A man was running down the street and disappeared between buildings. A car pulled away from the curb and raced down the road in the direction where he had seen the person run. He called police headquarters to inform them about the shooting and went back to bed.

When he arrived at the office, he had a message from Tom Peaks who said it was urgent to contact him immediately. "Jacob Schreiber here, Tom, what seems to be the problem?" the gumshoe asked.

Peaks said, "You remember when I talked to you at The Red Dahlia I mentioned some big ugly guy who walked out the back door with one of the musician? Well, he took some shots at me early this morning. I was walking home on Sunset when I heard tires squeal. I would say it was around three this morning. When I turned my head to look, I saw the face of the driver of the Caddy and it was him. I barely had time to duck and heard a shot go over my head. I ran as fast as I could and went into an alley where a car could not go and that probably saved my life. Within minutes, I heard police sirens close by and knew it was safe for me to resume my walk. You said you would help me if I cooperate. Well, Mr. Investigator, I'm ready."

"I'm glad you didn't get hurt or killed, Tom. You were lucky the cops were close by and probably heard the gun shots. A tree or two probably saved your life. Why don't you come to my office as soon as you can and I'll make the necessary arrangements for you. Good, see you in about an hour."

Jacob knew this was the right time for Lieutenant Jones to step in. He called the Homicide detective who was pleased to hear about a possible witness to the Carl Murdoch murder. Jones said he would be there in about forty minutes.

The parking lot attendant came up to Jacob's office to inquire why he was having a mechanic work on his car.

Anne's sixth sense told her there was something wrong going on. She ran from her desk to Jacob's office, entered without knocking and told him what the lot attendant had just said. Jacob was out of there like a jackrabbit, down the stairs in record time and out to where his car was parked. He saw a pickup truck leave the vicinity and his instinct told him danger was ahead. Jacob made a mental note of the truck and the name painted on it. He went to his car and saw that the hood had not been closed right. Always had a problem with the thing and never got around to having it fixed. He gently pulled the hood up and immediately saw the wiring hooked to the starter leading to some sticks of dynamite. As he was closing the hood, his peripheral vision told him someone was coming towards him. He gently but quickly pulled his .45 out and as he turned, saw the Lieutenant standing there with a surprised look on his face.

"We are sensitive this morning, are we not, Jacob?" Bill Jones said. "Did someone threaten you this early in the day," he inquired.

"Sorry about that, Lieutenant, let me show you. Someone would like me to fly to outer space," as he opened the hood of his car. "Now, would you not say that Mr. Profacini is really getting scared about something? For one thing, he wants to make sure I'm not around to find out what's bothering him."

"That is deadly business," the Lieutenant said. "I can see the seriousness of the situation. Let me go to my car and summon the bomb squad to relieve the pain," as Bill Jones hurried to his car less than a hundred feet away.

The two men stood around waiting for the LAPD explosive experts to arrive. Fortunately, the parking spaces around Jacob's car were not taken. The Lieutenant and Jacob prevented anyone from getting too close. Within twenty minutes, the explosive experts showed up. It took them less than five minutes to take away the dynamite. Jacob and the Lieutenant walked back to the second floor office where he told Anne about the incident. The lot attendant came rushing back in wondering why the police were all over the place. Jacob thanked him for rushing up to him about someone working on his car. It saved his life and probably others.

The lot attendant said, "I've got the license plate number and the name that was on the door, if that will help," as he handed a sheet of paper to Jacob.

The gumshoe took the occasion to introduce Lieutenant Jones to the lot attendant, who in turn told the detective he could park free at any time on his lot.

Jacob sat at his desk and was just about to make a telephone call when Anne walked in with coffee and doughnuts for him and the Lieutenant. He thanked her and asked if she would take messages for the next half-hour. He also mentioned he was expecting a gruffy-looking young man by the name of Tom Peaks to show up. He looked at the notes he had on Profacini, picked up the telephone and dialed. A male voice answered with the name of some business Jacob did not understand.

"This is Jacob Schreiber, could you put Vito Profacini on the line please, I have an urgent message for him." He waited what seemed to be a long two minutes then a voice came on and said: "This is Vito Profacini, Mr. Schreiber, what can I do for you?"

"It's what I can do for you, Vito, that will keep you alive. If you don't stop playing dynamite with me, you're going to regret the day you heard my name. It was a nice try with the old starter trick but it didn't work, Vito. Lieutenant Jones who is here with me had his experts remove it. If it's war you want, war you will get. Are we clear on that, Mr. Profacini?" There was a pause for a moment and Jacob picked up the conversation again. "You seem to forget I'm an ex-Marine and have a lot of friends that owe me from past favors. I want you to know, Vito, that I am not afraid of you or any of your men. As of tonight, some of your nightclubs may experience missing customers. I don't think they'll be able to deal with it as efficiently as I did with my dynamite problem. We are about three thousand ex-Marines itching for a little bit of action and always willing to help each other," Jacob concluded.

Vito Profacini said, "I'm sorry to hear you are so upset, Mr. Schreiber. I will find out who did this to you, and be assured they will be punished severely. There are no reasons for you and me to be at each other's throat. Could I invite you to lunch at my Fiore d'Italia and we can talk this over like two grown up men?"

Jacob thought for a moment and then told him he would be there with a friend at one o'clock today, then put the telephone down. "Well, Lieutenant, you and I are going to have Italian food for lunch today. How does that sound my, friend?"

"You're putting me on the spot, Jacob, but I don't mind. We cannot let this hoodlum think he can run things his way and scare us on top of it. Vito Profacini is close to falling into hot water, if you know what I mean," the homicide detective concluded.

Anne knocked on the door to let Jacob know Tom Peaks had arrived. The young man, looking a bit haggard walked in and sat in the empty chair. Jacob introduced him to the Lieutenant, then said, "I hope you don't mind if the Lieutenant sits in on the conversation with us, Tom."

Moving to adjust his seating position Tom appeared to be nervous, he could hardly sit still. "It's okay, Mr. Schreiber, I need to get this stuff off my chest before somebody succeeds in pumping bullets into me."

Jacob said, "Take your time, Tom, we're going to do everything we can to help you. I told the Lieutenant about our conversation at The Red Dahlia and informed him about the street incident this morning. Whenever you're ready and wherever you want to begin, it's fine. I'm sure that one or both of us will have questions for you at some point. Would you like a coffee and some doughnuts?"

Jacob walked out and asked Anne if she would fill the request.

By noontime, Jacob and the Lieutenant had enough information to pursue a thorough investigation and possibly bring a close to the Carl Murdoch murder case.

When the two arrived at the Italian restaurant, a Maître D' greeted them with an inquisitive look on his face. He immediately took them to a private seating area at the far end of the dining area. Vito Profacini got up to greet Jacob and did not appear surprised, at least he did not show it, to see the Lieutenant as he also greeted him. Both Jacob and the Lieutenant were suspicious of the motive behind the luncheon invitation. After the food was ordered, they waited for Vito to open the conversation. Open the conversation he did.

"I'm certainly disturbed by the fact someone is trying to do you harm, Mr. Schreiber. Since we last talked, I found out one of my men was not happy with the way you treated him in The Red Dahlia. I also understand he instigated the scuffle. He should have known that an ex-Marine trained as a commando is no pushover. Hiring someone to plant explosives under the hood of your car without my knowledge is something I don't tolerate. Don't get me wrong, if I had been informed of his intentions beforehand, I would have stopped him. Regardless, he's no longer in my employ and has been sent back to Italy. I'm a businessperson, Mr. Schreiber, and I don't need actions which will cause my business establishments to suffer. I'm offering both of you my cooperation and assure you that if anything is directed at you, Mr. Schreiber, it will not come from me or any members of my organization," concluded the Mafia don.

For a moment, Jacob looked at his friend then again at Profacini. He could tell the host was not comfortable and it was fine with him. "Mr. Profacini, since we are in a polite mode today, I appreciate what you're saying and hope it is the truth. The Lieutenant and I certainly appreciate your comments. Just so that you understand how I feel, Vito, I've been through a war and I'm not afraid to be involved in another. This time, since it would be on my turf and because I'm in charge of my own destiny I want you to know I can be very nasty. I prefer the peace side of things, so if it's going to be that way I'll leave it at that."

The silence was so intense you could hear a fly go by fifty feet away. It did not stay that way very long, people came in for lunch or a drink at the bar. Vito Profacini thanked his guests for coming in and emphasized all would be as he had said. He tried not to show his uneasiness, but it was clear to the Lieutenant that Jacob had made his point. For some reason, Bill Jones detected a sense of fear in the gangster's behavior. He wondered if the Mafia don feared the police or the private investigator more. The detective was happy he didn't have to say anything. His presence said it all.

On the way back to Jacob's office, the two friends talked intensely about their meeting with the head of organized crime in Southern California. Both agreed a point had been made, and both agreed not to let their guard down at any time. Trusting a gangster is the worst thing you can do as a law enforcement person. Jacob told his friend he would do everything possible to find something the DA could make stick in court.

From the earlier conversation they had with Tom Peaks, new leads had to be followed and new avenues investigated. The end of a second Mafia don was beginning to be believable. How soon it would happen, one had to hope: soon!

## CHAPTER SIXTEEN...

The office of Schreiber & Dombrowski Investigations was now located in a more modern building on Sunset Boulevard. A ground-floor location with more than twice the space the previous office had. Anne and Laura had handled the move on a Saturday to avoid any business disruptions. Extra furniture was bought, and this time Anne had her own private office.

Jacob wanted to ease her into the business as a full-time partner by giving her a variety of cases to work on. The first large account he assigned to her was a major Savings and Loan Corporation who had been hit by a well-organized swindle operation. This was the type of work which demanded meticulous scrutiny. Anne was good at it.

Clouds mixed with sunshine had been the forecast for the week ahead in the City of Angels. Jacob was going where the oil refineries were located in Long Beach. This kind of weather was perfect for surveillance. After his dinner meeting with Graham Longhaul, he had information that would help him identify the vandals and do something about it. The private eye was almost sure it was an inside job. It could be a disgruntled employee not happy with the denial of a request for a pay raise. In a situation where vandalism hits at different times in different locations, it could also be the work of organized labor or worse, organized crime. The gumshoe had been informed that a tanker belonging to Longhaul's firm would be unloading its cargo this morning. He had the name of the ship's Captain and members of the crew. He also had a land contact person who would be responsible for the unloading. All he needed to do was to find out from the dock foreman where and when the Texas oil was being unloaded. When he got to the refinery, Jacob had to report to the head of security. As he walked in the security area, the name on the door was not foreign to him. William G. Cox had a familiar sound to the gumshoe. He remembered a Marine from his unit who had been wounded and did not want to go back home. A tough guy he was, this Bill Cox.

The head of security got up from behind his desk and opened the door to let Jacob come in. Cox stopped in his tracks. He could not believe what he was seeing. Could this be the same Jacob Schreiber who had been with him fighting the Japanese in the South Pacific? The two men looked stunned. They shook hands, smiled and could not stop telling the other how pleased they were to meet again. It took a few minutes until things settled down and Bill Cox asked his secretary to bring coffee for his visitor. He told Jacob how he jumped on the job offer the day after he was discharged from the Marines. "What's this I see? You are a private investigator?" said the security man. "I remember you talking about doing that once the war was over. I'm glad to see you've followed through, Jacob."

Jacob said, "It was a struggle at first, Bill, but I got lucky. My business has grown so much in the last six months, I can hardly keep up with it. I do have a strong partner and things are looking up. I'm here today at the request of a new client, a Graham Longhaul from Texas. From the look on your face, I see you recognize the name. He has a cargo ship that's suppose to be unloading here this morning. My main reason for being here is that Mr. Longhaul has had some vandalism done to his equipment. In the past month, at least a dozen of his trucks carrying fuel across several states, have been hit by acts of vandalism such as slashed tires. In one case, the tanker was punctured and the fuel let out. This can turn into a very ugly situation if I don't find the culprits real soon. I could use your help to guide me around this plant and the loading docks," Jacob concluded.

"You're right, Jacob, vandalism in the oil industry can be dangerous and deadly, not to mention filthy dirty and a hazard to bird sanctuaries. To make it easier I'll take you around myself," said the former Marine.

When the gumshoe left the refinery some four hours later, he had a possible lead which pointed towards extortion of some kind. Jacob thought it would not be unusual for someone to target a rich oil producer. Furthermore, if that oil producer happened to have a weakness somewhere in his operation or perhaps his private life, this could make it a whole lot easier for the party doing the extortion. Again, he thought about the first time he met Graham Longhaul. To Jacob's keen sense of observation, there did not appear to be anything in Mr. Longhaul's demeanor which would bring to the forefront some character flaw. He remembered the conversation being totally concentrated on business. First, it was the truck fleet, then the floating tankers he owned. All at once, it struck Jacob that his new client never talked about his personal life. Usually people who face or fear danger of some kind have a tendency to speak about their family. Graham Longhaul did not. Now it became important to the private eye to find out about his client's private activities. The answer or at least the clues to finding out why this man's company was being targeted could very well be in his private affairs. So many thoughts, so many angles and always the same answer; no answer.

When Jacob arrived at the office, several telephone messages were waiting for him. Laura Brown mentioned Lieutenant Jones had said it was urgent.

"Lieutenant, this is Jacob. I just got back from Long Beach. Didn't get lucky yet but at least there were no major problems when I was there. What's on your mind?" the gumshoe asked.

"You're not going to like what you are about to hear, my friend. Earlier today, Tom Peaks called me to let me know he was on his way to my office. He never made it. An hour or so after his call I was informed about the gunning down of a man at Western and Santa Monica. It turned out to be young Tom. I guess his fears were justified when he last spoke with us. Witnesses said someone in an old Chevy fired from the passenger side. We had a good description of the car. It happened, yes you guessed it, to be a reported stolen car from last night. We found it five blocks away from where the shooting occurred. In the car, we did find something that may help us in our investigation. The ashtray contained three old cigarette butts, one of which was a French brand, Gauloise if I'm not mistaken. You know the kind that really stinks up the air when you smoke them? The car reeked of the odor. The owner of the car does not smoke so that does give us something to go on. Maybe one of Profacini's boys has a penchant for French flavor."

Jacob said, "I'm not surprised that Tom Peaks was eliminated. He knew too much about what happened at The Red Dahlia when Carl Murdoch was gunned down. Our witness is gone, Lieutenant, but that won't stop me from digging further. I do have a hunch on Murdoch's case, but hunches don't convince juries. Thanks for the information, Lieutenant, I'll be in touch in the morning. Got to go to a ball game tonight."

Jacob just sat there thinking about Tom Peaks, a young drug addict who was reaching for help and was done in by the mob. *Someone will have to pay for that*, the private eye thought. Now would be the time to ask his Federal friend for a favor. He picked up the telephone and dialed Special Agent Ryle's number. After a brief conversation, he got him to agree to meet with him at The Red Dahlia for a drink. Jacob had it all figured out in his mind. If his idea worked, he could have a final answer on the Murdoch case before the day was over. He then proceeded to finish writing his notes on the refinery surveillance, folded the three pages, placed them in an envelope and walked over to Laura's desk.

"Could you place this envelope in the Longhaul file?" he asked his newly inducted secretary. "Would you return this call and tell Mr. Longhaul I will be happy to meet with him tomorrow when he gets here. Has everything gone okay with you so far, Laura? Don't be afraid to ask if something appears to be confusing. I have a habit of keeping too much information in my head instead of writing it down for the file. I'm going to meet with the Lieutenant and the FBI Special agent in West LA for a drink, and then I'm going to the ballpark to play with my kids. Any messages between now and the time you go home, you can leave on my desk. See you tomorrow," Jacob said with a smile as he was hurrying out the door.

When Jacob got to The Red Dahlia, Special Agent Don Ryle was sitting in a booth by himself sipping a cold beer. The gumshoe joined him and ordered a round of drinks including one for the Lieutenant who had just walked in. The bartender knew who they were and tried to pass the drinks on the house but Jacob refused and paid for everyone. "Next time," he had told the barkeep, "it will be on you."

The three law enforcement friends chitchatted for a while until Jacob brought the conversation to a more serious side.

The private eye said, "Well guys, our witnesses keep getting bumped off. We have to be better at protecting them or no one will want to associate with us. I know that Profacini is behind this. He'll play it his way for a time, thinking he has us all fooled. Maybe it's time for the good guys to get in the ballgame and show these Mafiosos what we are made of. I have a plan that may trip them into thinking they have us on a string. What they won't know is that we planted the string and can pull it tight at any time. In order to make this plan work, I'm going to need your cooperation. Yes, both of you will have to pull some strings of your own, which I know you can."

Both Don Ryle and Bill Jones had raised eyebrows. The Lieutenant even picked up Jacob's beer to look at it as if some strange potion had been added to it causing him to be acting so weird. Once the kidding was over, they were ready for a serious conversation.

Jacob laid out his plan as well as he could. From the intense look on his face, the private eye was convinced his maneuver would work. Convincing his friends to set a trap for Vito Profacini was not difficult. What would not be so easy, was to make it legal for the DA to endorse. Sting operations were not preferred tactics by District Attorneys who had to answer to higher political heads. After another round of drinks the plan even looked better.

"Jacob," said the Lieutenant, "are you sure you can find a solid informer to put the wheels of this plan in motion? A guy who would not be afraid to take the risk. You know, if the story failed, this informer could find himself feeding the sharks somewhere in the Pacific Ocean."

"I do," Jacob said. "But, it's not a guy, it's a girl. She's a very good con person. Lily is her name. You remember Lily, Lieutenant, you helped me get her out of incarceration about a year ago. She was a fraud artist and a good one at that. She said she would repay me the favor whenever a situation would arise. Well, the situation has arrived, gentlemen."

The two police officers looked stunned.

"A woman," they both said at the same time, "just impossible."

Don Ryle further said, "This is far too dangerous for a woman. We need a man with nerves of steel to handle what you want. In my years of law enforcement with the FBI, I have never heard of such a bold approach. We're dealing with guys who would kill their mother over a spilled cup of coffee here. No, Jacob, I haven't met the woman who could outsmart a guy like Profacini. Don't forget, my friend, this Mafioso we're talking about is going to be charged with counterfeiting. He's smart, and besides, he has the best criminal lawyers in the country. Now, how do you think some floozy from Hollywood Boulevard is going to deal with him?"

Lieutenant Jones was just sitting there grinning, thinking about the time he met Lily. *Jacob is right*, he thought. *If there is a person, any person who can pull the wool over Vito Profacini's eyes, Lily is that person.*

# CHAPTER SEVENTEEN

When Laura Brown arrived at the office earlier than usual, she was surprised to see a woman leaning on the doorframe. She appeared to be in her late twenties. Her hair looked as if it had not seen the inside of a salon recently. As she approached the door, she was cautious to keep her eyes on the woman. "Is there something I can do for you?" Laura asked the woman.

"You could open the door so I could sit down and wait for Jacob to show up. I'm Lily and I understand he's been looking for me."

Laura remembered her boss talking about this woman recently. Well, whatever reason he had to be looking for her did not seem personal. She proceeded to open the door and let Lily in at the same time. "I'm Laura. Take a seat, Lily, and I'll have coffee ready in a jiffy. Hope you haven't been waiting too long. Mr. Schreiber mentioned you might be showing up soon. Anything else I can get for you?" Laura asked in her professional way.

Lily did not bother answering Laura's question. She just sat there with her eyes closed, as if in a deep concentration. The coffee was almost ready when the office door opened wide and in walked a cheerful gumshoe.

Jacob exclaimed, "Well, good morning, Lily. I see you got my message. Good morning, Laura, a bit early this morning, aren't you?" the private eye said.

"Well, Jacob, I had to take my car in for an oil change and tune-up and it's only three blocks from the office." Then she added, "Glad I came in early, so Miss Lily did not have to wait outside too long. The coffee is ready whenever you want some." Laura looked in Lily's direction and saw she had her eyes open. She offered her a cup of coffee and proceeded next door to get the boss's favorite doughnuts.

Jacob had found Lily through an informer he had been using from the first day he opened his office. She had been located in a safe house for former prostitutes where she worked and helped other women in the same situation she had found herself when Jacob rescued her. She was totally off drugs and booze. A bit over a year it was since that day when she had decided that enough bad treatment at the hands of a pimp was enough. It happened on Hollywood Boulevard late at night. Jacob was walking home from his office when he noticed this couple ahead of him, arguing loudly and the man slapping the woman across the face as hard as he could. He never had time to rush to her help. She had pulled a knife from nowhere and stabbed the guy in the chest. As he fell to the pavement, she stabbed him again and again. The woman then moved back to lean against a store window, knife in hand dripping with the dead man's blood. As Jacob approached, the woman started to speak at such a fast pace it was difficult to understand what she was trying to say. In any event Jacob called the Lieutenant from the pay telephone at the corner and waited with the woman for him to arrive. It was obvious this woman was in total shock.

Distressed over what had just happened, the gumshoe knew how terribly mistreated some of these street workers were by pimps who only cared about the money side of things. Because he had been a witness to the whole situation, he was able to help this woman with her plea of self-defense. He also helped her find work with a group of friends who had a safe house for woman wanting to get off the street and away from the pimps. That woman was Lily. Jacob had made a friend of her and helped her enroll in an acting school where she would learn a different trade than the one she had been practicing. She had always told the private eye she would be available to help him anytime he wanted her to. Well, now was the time, and there she was.

"I'm here Jacob, somewhat tired because I had to be on my feet most of the night with a couple of new arrivals at the house, if you know what I mean. One girl had a broken jaw, the other's face was so bruised and swollen, you would have thought a truck had hit her. It sounded urgent, so here I am," Lily said.

"Thanks for coming in, Lily. I have a contract for you. I can see the surprised look on your tired face, but trust me. If you decide to do what I have in mind, you'll make a fast two grand. Besides, you'll be able to practice your acting skills at the same time. It would be dangerous for someone without street smarts, but for you I have a feeling it will be a piece of cake." Jacob went on to tell Lily what he had in mind. After three cups of coffee and as many doughnuts, an hour of uninterrupted talk had passed. Lily didn't look as tired any more. The coffee had revived her, but most likely Jacob's plan of action had excited her more than the coffee.

"You see, Lily, I believe this plan can be completed in two sessions at the most. Furthermore, you'll have the FBI and me in the background protecting you. I'm fully aware that these mobsters are dangerous but they have to be stopped. If we don't stop them, more people will become addicted to heroin and whatever else, and more people will die. Together we can make a difference, Lily. We need your help. Tell me if you're up to doing this. I need to know now and act fast. Ships are coming in almost every week with tons of dope for distribution nation-wide. Your real name, for that matter, your real face will never be given to the press or anyone else. Only I and the FBI will know who you really are." Jacob concluded.

Lily was fidgety, restless, shifting her weight in the chair, staring straight ahead with a poker face on. She slammed the arm of the chair so hard it startled Jacob. Lily stood up and the gumshoe thought his plan had just been flushed away.

He was just about to say something when she exclaimed: "Damn it! If you're not the most convincing gumshoe anyone has ever encountered. I'll do it, Jacob, on one condition. I don't want anything for me, but would prefer you make a donation to the safe house I work at. We need the money for medication and treatment of these poor girls who come to us half dead and many times on the verge of committing suicide. If you agree to that, I'll do it," the former prostitute concluded.

After Lily had left the office, Jacob called Anne and Laura to bring them up to date on the very special initiative he was to undertake. He informed his two trusted associates about the plan to have a sting operation aimed directly at bringing down Vito Profacini's business and solving the murder of Carl Murdoch at the same time. As this operation was going to be so intense, he wanted to make sure they both understood the danger Lilly would be placing herself in if any of this information was to leak out to the wrong people. By that, he meant the press first, then the organized crime group headed by don Vito.

He told his partner Anne and his secretary Laura that Lily had willingly volunteered to do this. As far as he was concerned, she was the only person who could bring it to a successful end. Lily had seen it all, he told them. Nine years on the streets of LA as a prostitute, pusher and addict more than qualified her for the job. The inner sanctuary of the Mafia was not an easy nut to crack. If anyone could penetrate this group without causing any suspicion, Lily was the one. The only hick in the whole situation was that it had to be done fast. No time to build credibility with the gangsters, almost like a hit and run. In fact, it was a hit and run. That's how Jacob thought about his plan. Get in there, get the information you need and get out. He laid out the plan so the women would understand what to do in case there was a hitch somewhere.

Both women were trained on the use of a handgun and were licensed to carry a hidden revolver. Anne had said on many occasions she would not hesitate to use her gun should the situation arise. She and Laura had been to the practice range on a regular weekly basis.

Jacob did not think of anything to add until the time came to make the move on the Red Dahlia. Everyone knew the FBI would be there as well as a couple of undercover officers from Lieutenant Jones's department. The whole group would meet at Jacob's office the day before the sting set-up. This way there was no danger of tripping over each other and claiming jurisdiction. For the time being, it was a question of keeping an eye on the bar patrons.

The gumshoe was good at his game. He called his friend Geoff who happened to be one of the top make-up artists at MGM's studios. He needed him to do a job on Lilly and on himself. He figured a different haircut, some make-up and a new wardrobe would make him almost unrecognizable in the dim light of a bar. Two of Vito's boys were regulars at the Red Dahlia. They were trying to intimidate the barman-manager into paying protection money like the one before him did. Rodney Spikes was not an easy guy to push around. An ex-police officer and former golden glove lightweight champion is no pushover at any time, gun or no gun. The two goons knew that and were careful not to squeeze him too hard. They probably thought patience would win him over. Vito Profacini, their boss, had been informed that the owner of the establishment was the aunt of the District Attorney. Jacob figured that to avoid harassment the mobster told his guys to lay back and not use the normal approach. The bar was no doubt a rendezvous place for pushers, loan sharks and all these other good professions associated with the underworld. What it also had was a link to a ring specializing in counterfeiting. That link was the key to Profacini's weakness and possibly his arraignment as an accomplice in the murder of one Carl Murdoch.

These were all thoughts and angles Jacob was throwing around in his head hoping it would give him the answers he needed.

One of Vito's goons by the name of Tony was the one Jacob suspected of being the hitman in Murdoch's case. He hung around the Red Dahlia four to five times a week. He always sat in the same booth where he could be close to the jazz trio. Many times one or all of the musicians would sit with him and have a drink. What the connection was between them, Jacob did not know yet but he was doing his best to find out.

Four undercover officers, two from the FBI and two from the LAPD homicide division, Lily, unrecognizable from the last time she had visited Jacob's office, all met to lay out the last strategy in this sting operation. There was no turning back now. The wheels were in motion and the momentum was being felt by all. The group looked like the cast for a theater play. The only difference; this was real life and the only one in risk of losing was Lilly. She was conscious of that and said so at the meeting. As long as these men would be there, in the club, she said she had total confidence.

Jacob went over the plan once more. He handed Lily three of the counterfeit bills that she immediately put in her wallet. She had been provided with a false driver's license and a false passport. In order for the sting operation to succeed, everyone involved had to play his or her part to perfection. The gum-shoe would have been a great teacher. He just loved doing this kind of work and showing people how easy it can be if the scenario is followed to the letter.

Jacob said, "We all know what each of us has to do. Let's make sure nothing is left out. I thank every one of you for being so cooperative and especially you, Lilly. Let's do it folks." Everyone had their own transportation and they went on their way to West Los Angeles and The Red Dahlia.

**CHAPTER EIGHTEEN...**

Jacob loved the involvement he had with the Little League. This gave him an opportunity to mingle with children and their parents. This social outlet gave him an occasion to see the good side of life. He needed that change of pace to keep his sanity. Investigative work can be very rewarding financially but could become a disaster emotionally. Dealing with the criminal mind is a challenge in itself. Doing it on a regular basis can be draining to a point of no return. One needs an outlet where real people bring a balance to his or her life. The last little league practice had been extra good as Jacob told the kids and parents at hot dog time. Everyone was doing better. With children nine and ten years old, patience was the key, and repetition made them grasp what teamwork and the game of baseball was all about.

The ringing of the telephone brought his attention back to the present.

"Schreiber here," he answered. "Well, Lieutenant, I didn't think I would hear from you until tomorrow. Anything special you have in mind?" Jacob asked.

"I sure do, Jacob," said the homicide detective. "One of The Sons of God who had been let out on bail was found dead in the Mexican area of downtown LA. His throat was slashed and he received a bullet through the forehead. Someone wanted to make sure he would not talk anymore. We received a call about the dead body around seven tonight. Where the killing occurred we don't know, but our medical examiner tells us he had been dead a few hours since rigor mortis had already began to set in. An informer gave us a license plate number and the make of a car. The last unusual thing about this murder victim you would never guess, Jacob!"

Jacob said, "Knowing the man was part of Joey Durango's gang I would not even attempt to guess what you're about to tell me, Lieutenant."

"As unusual as this may sound to you, Jacob, the man was carrying some counterfeit bills in his wallet along with an old business card of yours. It even had your private line number and new office address written on the back of it. Does this ring a bell with you?" the Lieutenant asked.

"The only time I can recall writing my new address and private line number on the back of one of my old cards is when I gave one to Tom Peaks some weeks back. How did this guy get my card in his possession? Could he be the one who killed Tom, and then for whatever reason, was himself eliminated?

That's the only plausible answer I can come up with, Lieutenant," Jacob said.

"What you say makes sense to me, Jacob. We do have a set of prints that needs to be identified from the Peaks case. If they match, then he's the one that killed him. The Profacini boys most likely eliminated him since he was not part of their ongoing plans. Just got a make on the car seen in East LA. There was no reason for me to think this car had not been stolen. It was, actually near where you live. I don't think we'll find any fresh prints in this one. Let's meet in the morning for coffee, if you're up to it, my friend," the homicide detective concluded.

Jacob just sat there spinning his thoughts on the latest event. For some reason, it kept bringing him back to The Red Dahlia. There has to be a strong connection amongst the bar patrons that he had missed. *Maybe we're all looking at the wrong side of the equation and none of us is seeing the real devil amongst the stack of angels.* His thinking just kept on working. Suppose it was not someone associated with organized crime that killed Carl Murdoch. Just a wild thought, but in this business, you cannot overlook anything. He thought, *I'm going to have to spend some more time listening to jazz for a while. Then he thought about his sting operation. Two days from now would probably be a good time to bring all the participants together again. His thoughts were moving again. What if Murdoch was eliminated for a totally different reason than what the police and have been talking about? The question is, for what other reason than knowing too much about the counterfeiting operation about to happen? What if someone seized the opportunity to do away with Carl Murdoch knowing the Profacini gang would be blamed for it? What if Tom Peaks had been mislead-ing us too? That could be a possibility,* he thought, *but whom would he have been covering for? Open-ing up these different angles would certainly compli-cate the investigation or would it?* He decided to get dressed and take a drive to West Los Angeles. An hour or so spent in the Red Dahlia may bring clarity to his thoughts.

When he got there the band was playing and the noise factor was at a high level. Jacob sat at the bar and ordered a beer. Once his eyes were accus-tomed to the dim lights, he saw a few faces he rec-ognized. Lilly in her new disguise was sitting in a booth with one of Profacini's goons. They appeared to be in an intense conversation. In the booth next to them were the two FBI agents and a young woman sitting with them. Wow! He thought to himself, the crew is doing their homework. As he turned around, he noticed the two undercover homicide officers at a table nearby. *I guess I made the right decision by coming here*, Jacob thought. He ordered a second beer and went to sit at a corner table where he could have a view of the whole bar scene. None of the people he recognized, although he looked at them directly, acknowledged him. That was good because in setting up a sting operation you didn't want to make your presence known. He now focused his attention on the musicians, but kept an eye on the rest of the customers. At one point, he noticed a patron whom he had not seen in there before, whisper to the bartender who then looked in his direction shaking his head in a negative way. Whatever it was the man had said or asked, he did not get the response he expected and went back to join his two friends at a table. From his vantage point, Jacob could also see who was coming in and going out of the premises. The door leading to the alley where Murdoch had been killed was locked so no patron could go through there. He saw a few individuals coming in go directly to a table where Profacini's boys were, make an exchange of some kind and leave. He was sure these were drug pushers making their payoff. Then he noticed something unusual when the band took a break. The piano player looked in the direction of the goons' table, quickly glanced at Jacob and hurried towards the main entrance door. He was immediately followed by the largest of the goons whom he heard others call Tony. Now there was something going on here, but he was not going to give his hand away so he stayed put. In less than five minutes the odd couple were back inside walking to their destination pretending not to know each other. Tim Huckles visited the men's room and then returned to his piano. Jacob had seen enough. It was time for him to move on and he did. As he walked towards his car, he had the feeling someone was following him. He made a quick turn at the next corner and waited for his follower. He didn't have to wait long. In seconds, the goon showed up frantically looking for Jacob. Hiding in the entrance of a corner store, he could not be seen unless you turned your head completely to the left. When Tony did so, he got a mouthful of hard knuckles and fell to the ground. Before he could even get up and move his hand inside his jacket, Jacob had his own .45 out pointing directly at the man's head. "I wouldn't move a hair if I were you. I have an itchy finger when it comes to being followed at night. Turn on your face with your arms above your head so I can see them," Jacob said.

The man didn't dare make the smallest motion. His mouth was bleeding from the punch he had just received. Jacob frisked him and removed a Luger and hunting knife from the man's Jacket. "I have a good notion to plug you right where you are. What's your name, so that I know who to send the remains to? You had better believe I'm serious. Doing away with the likes of you is no worse than stepping on a cockroach. I'm not going to wait all night for you to answer me, fellow. Once more, I know who you work for, what's your name?"

"I'm Jack the Ripper for you, flatfoot. I don't think you have the guts to shoot me anyway," the man concluded. Just as he finished his sentence Jacob pointed his .45 at the man's back and let a shot go near him. The sound was deafening and caused the goon to squirm.

"So, now you know I have guts, the next one will be aimed more to the center, that's right, in your private little parts. One last time, what's your name?" Jacob asked.

Realizing Jacob meant business the man said, "You'll be sorry for that. My name is Antonio Privanti. Everyone calls me Tony. Mr. Profacini is going to deal with you." Thinking that the mention of Southern California's godfather would intimidate the gumshoe, Tony made a move to turn around. The reaction from the private eye was fast. A quick kick to the head made him see there was no fooling this man. "Okay," said the Mafia enforcer, "what is it you want?"

"It's not what I want Tony," Jacob said. "It's more like what I'm going to tell you, and you better listen well if you want to live longer. I'm going to ask you one question, if you give me the right answer you can get up and leave. If you don't give me the right answer, I'm going to tie you up to this telephone pole without any clothes on, pour honey all over you and let the ants tickle you for a while. Does that sound like a good deal Tony?" The man did not utter a sound. He was either ignoring Jacob totally or thinking how he could get himself out of this situation. Maybe if he stalled long enough he thought, one of his buddies would come out looking for him. On the other hand, he had not told anyone he was coming back to the bar and figured this crazy gumshoe would do exactly what he said he would do. "What's your question, flatfoot?"

Jacob said, "I want to know what you and the piano player talked about when you went outside with him. Now, that is a legitimate question and I would advise you not to lie to me Tony!"

The uncomfortable gangster thought for a moment, then asked Jacob if he could sit up. The answer was negative. "Tim, that's the piano player, and me had a deal going with this Josh character before he got busted. We thought we could move some phony bills around without Vito knowing about it. We have been skimming from the drug pushers, but you had to come along and spoil the fun. Poking your nose in and out of the bar scares the druggies away. When he saw you tonight, he wanted me to do you in. This is why I followed you here."

"You can sit up now, Tony," Jacob said. That's when Tony noticed another man standing behind Jacob. Not being able to clearly see who it was and thinking it was one of his friends, he made a move to grab the gun from Jacob's hand. Bad mistake, Tony felt the lights going out and a terrible pain pounding inside his head. Jacob had foreseen he would attempt to do just that and was ready for him. With a jab like force, he had hit Tony on the side of the head with his heavy-duty .45. Blood was streaming down the man's face and he softly rolled on his side unaware of his surroundings.

"That, my friend, was one hell of a good jab," Lieutenant Jones said. "I heard his answer to your question, but as we both know it would not stand up in court. However, since we now know more than we did about this musician, we can put a tail on him immediately. I'll arrange to keep this sleeping beauty," referring to Tony Privanti, "out of the way for a week or two."

"Thanks for being there, Bill. This guy had no clue you were standing in the dark, and when he realized someone was standing behind me, he thought it was one of his own gang, and decided to make a move. Bad judgment on his part, wouldn't you say Lieutenant?"

## CHAPTER NINETEEN...

The early morning had been a hectic one at Jacob Schreiber's office. First, the false alarm fire followed by the LAPD special bomb squad who rushed in to evacuate the building. The call to police headquarters had come from a disturbed mental patient of a shrink who had his office on the third floor of the building. The disruptions lasted until eleven. By then, the telephone was ringing off the hook.

Anne had been working hard on the bank fraud dossier. For the time being, she had succeeded in putting a lid on the problem of skimming money from wealthy clients' accounts. It had reached to the level of a branch vice-president. In all, she had uncovered nine people in five different branches actively defrauding the bank for millions of dollars. The Board of Directors had been so pleased with the work performed by Anne, they decided to allow a substantial monthly retainer fee for the next twelve months. This way it would help higher management keep an eye on employees they suspected of possibly committing fraud.

In their weekly meeting, Jacob had nothing but praise for Anne's work. Now that she had successfully completed the major part of the bank's fraud case, it was time for a new assignment. There was no lack of work since the office was continually swamped with requests from the movie studios and major corporations. Schreiber, in the short time he had been in the private eye business, had built a strong reputation. A combination of honesty and guts with the constant willingness to pursue clues other investigators would not bother with, made him and his agency stand tall against the competition. Not a two-week period went by without some licensed investigator wanting to join Jacob's team. In his mind, expansion was fine as long as the workload was there. At the present time, the three of them could handle it all. Jacob always said you should not wear yourself thin because that's when you make fatal mistakes. He could see the need to have an extra investigator or two for a short period. For the time being, he preferred working a little harder and if in a bind, hire a competent PI on a contractual basis. This way he could test the abilities of a few and possibly choose the best of the lot anytime he wanted to.

Jacob was going over his notes on the Longhaul file when there was a knock on his door. Laura Brown came in to tell him a suspicious, tough and heavy looking man was waiting to see him in the outer office. He had told Laura to inform Mr. Schreiber it was private and urgent. "Bring him in," Jacob said.

The man walked in. He was huge. Laura had not exaggerated. Three hundred pounds, to say the least. Even an experienced former Marine like Jacob looked a little surprised. The big man sat across from him.

"My name is André," he said. André Felipapa. Everyone calls me Tiny. I used to work for Vito Profacini's brother in Italy. I came to New York in 1935 with my parents, and we moved to California two years later. After high school, I began a feed business. You know, feed for farm animals. Mainly horses. I did not want to take part in Mr. Profacini's type of work. He's a bad man, Mr. Schreiber. His brother Frank was the opposite. He was killed during a family feud. I heard stories about people disappearing never to be found again. People associated with Mr. Vito kept coming to my feed store wanting me to work with them. I refused, and they left, threatening me. They said they would come back and I would be sorry. I need your help, Mr. Schreiber. A friend who works in the DA's office told me I could trust you with my life."

"Slow down, Tiny." Jacob could not remember his last name for the moment. "I hear what you are saying, but this is more for the police to look into than it is for me. Profacini is on the black list with the LAPD, so if you make an official complaint I'm almost positive they'll do something about it," the private eye concluded.

"Don't get me wrong, Mr. Schreiber, I'm not scared for myself. I just worry about my wife and children. These people, from what I know, have no respect for human life. I have money to pay you," as he pulled out a large envelope from inside his jacket and placed it on Jacob's desk. "There is two thousand dollars of my hard-earned money in there. I just don't want anything to happen to my family. I have four children, the oldest is twelve and she wants to become a doctor."

Jacob could see the man was very upset. His eyes were moist. "I did not say I would not help you, Mr., I'm sorry what did you say your last name was?"

The gentle giant answered "Felipapa, André Felipapa."

"Mr. Felipapa I need more information from you," Jacob said.

The new client spent another forty minutes answering Jacob's questions and continually repeating he was concerned for his wife and children. The gumshoe promised him he would be by his place of business later that day. After he left, Jacob asked Anne to come talk to him. He wanted her to follow up on some information he had picked up at the Long Beach Refinery. Maybe she could get an itinerary of Longhaul's truck fleet with the names of every driver and all the personal information she could get on each one of them. Having Anne involved on the case would allow him to verify the problem his new client was having with the Profacini family.

The feed barn was on Ventura Boulevard just past Woodland Hills. Jacob looked around to familiarize himself. He was just walking by stacks of bales of hay when he noticed two men walking in. He remembered the shorter of the two from the Red Dahlia in West LA. From where he was standing, they could not see him. The taller one had a newspaper in his hands and Jacob quickly realized the man was going to put a match to it and torch the barn. He didn't give him a chance to do it. He jumped in the aisle with his .45 pointing at them. The short guy reached in his pocket and pulled out a gun. That was the last move he would ever make. Jacob's shot hit him right between the eyes. The taller man dropped the paper and made a move to retrieve his gun. This time the gumshoe hit him in the shoulder and sent him spinning and down to the dirt floor. He yelled at the man not to go for the inside of his jacket, but he did not listen and Jacob had no choice but to shoot him when he saw him pull a 9mm from inside his jacket. The noise of the gunshots brought a handful of onlookers to the barn. Jacob asked Tiny to get the people out of the way and to make sure no one touched anything. He went to the telephone and called Lieutenant Jones.

A half-hour later the Lieutenant showed up with an extra police car and the coroner's meat wagon. "Well, Jacob," Bill Jones said, "you can tell me all about it over a cup of coffee. I saw a sidewalk café a block and a half from here. I don't think there's anything more either of us can do here. I have been looking for this little guy for some time. He's been seen near crime scenes quite often lately. I guess I won't have the opportunity to question him about it. Believe me, Jacob, you did society a big favor today. Both of these guys had warrants issued on them for murders committed in the past two months. Only Profacini will miss them, but we'll deal with him, won't we?" concluded the homicide detective.

"As a matter of fact, Lieutenant, I think we should pay a visit to the godfather this very day. If you have the time that is," said the private eye.

After making sure the barn was safe from other intruders, Jacob went looking for Tiny. He found him inside the small building that served as an office. Jacob waited until he was done with his customer. "I don't think you will have any more problems for a while, Mr. Felipapa," the gumshoe said. "Tomorrow I'll bring you back your deposit. Since my work for you took such little time, consider it a trial session free of any compensation. I spoke with the Lieutenant and he agreed with me about posting some men here and at your home for a few days. He and I are going to have a private conversation with Vito

Profacini concerning the harassment you've been subjected to recently. Our methods are usually adhered to when presented verbally face to face. No, André, it is not necessary for you to pay me anything. When I get myself a horse, you can help me set up whatever is needed for his daily routine. Is that agreeable with you, my big man?" Jacob concluded.

"My friend in the DA's office was not wrong about you, Mr. Schreiber. You are a man who stands up for justice and the underdog. On behalf of my family, I thank you for protecting us," Tiny said.

When the Lieutenant and Jacob arrived at Vito Profacini's residence, a guard held them at the gate until Vito himself showed up to met them.

"Come in, gentlemen. What may I ask brings both of you for a visit? Please follow me to the study, we'll be more comfortable there to talk," said the Mafia headman.

They walked through the massive oak door, the flooring of the entrance hall was of marble. Jacob thought it had to have been imported from Italy. The walls were covered with older paintings, some of them depicting Jesus with his apostles and a tremendous large scene of the Last Supper. The study was a wall to wall bookshelf filled with books of all sorts. On the wall behind the desk, stuffed animal heads hung proudly. When one looked directly in the eyes of a prairie buffalo, you could almost feel him coming towards you. The desk itself was of massive proportion to go with the ego of the owner. It was made of beautiful cherry wood and shined like a star in the sky. The furniture was of leather, and there was plenty of it. What looked like, and probably was, an Oriental rug covered most of the room Vito had referred to as his study.

"Could I offer you gentlemen a drink or is it still duty time?" the smooth talking gangster said.

"Not at the moment for us, we are here on official business, Mr. Profacini, and it is not pleasant business at that," Lieutenant Jones said. "My friend Jacob was assaulted by two of your goons this afternoon. Unfortunately for them, they came out at the wrong end of the barn, so to speak. A tall one named Frankie and his usual partner in crime, little Joe, has departed for the Promised Land. I can see by the look in your face the news didn't make it to you before we got here. To make a long story short, let's just say they both pulled a gun, I would assume with intent to shoot at Mr. Schreiber a couple of hours ago. It is a case of self-defense, as you know. Besides, Jacob Schreiber is a licensed private investigator authorized to carry a concealed weapon. The incident happened while the gumshoe here was performing surveillance for a client of his. Furthermore, Mr. Profacini, some three weeks ago you had promised both of us that any members of your staff would not harass Jacob. That has not happened yet and I don't expect you'll keep your promise anyway," the Lieutenant concluded.

Profacini looked stunned. He tried to smile, but it came out more like a smirk. For once the Mafia don was fidgety as if something was really bothering him. He took a deep breath, opened a cigar box, and offered his guests who declined, then lit one for himself. After a couple of puffs Vito said, "I will keep my promise to you, Lieutenant, and you, Mr. Schreiber. What bothers me is that my nephew Joseph was stupid enough to pull a gun, like you said, on Jacob Schreiber. My sister is going to be very upset about the situation. If you don't mind may I suggest that we keep the details of this incident between ourselves? I'll make up something to the family, this way we'll avoid involving Mr. Schreiber and possibly causing him more concerns than he needs to have."

"This is okay with us, Vito," the homicide detective said. "Just make sure you keep your side of the bargain. My promise to you, Mr. Profacini, is very simple, don't let anything happen to my friend Jacob or to the owner of the barn in Malibu, a Mr. Felipapa. If it does, I'm coming after you full force," Jones concluded.

Like a good host, Vito escorted his two guests to the gate. The guard on duty did not know what to make of it so he just smiled as the Lieutenant and the private eye got into the unmarked police car. Profacini walked back to his house. The two lawmen could hear him swear in Italian and saw him shake his head in a negative motion.

## CHAPTER TWENTY...

You cannot always take the easy road in the private investigating business. It so happens there are times when the going is difficult to say the least. Such was the Carl Murdoch case. The police seemed to think he was eliminated because of non-payment of drugs. The LAPD had closed the file on this one. Except for a stubborn Lieutenant detective and a tenacious private investigator, the victim would have been forgotten a long time ago. Classified in peoples' minds as 'just another drug user we don't have to worry about.'

Jacob was reminiscing about his business. He sometimes wanted to reassure himself that what he was doing was the right type of work for him. On different occasions, having to fight for his life brought him back to the days of his tour of duty in the South Pacific not so many years back. He really did not enjoy the rough stuff, but knew it came with the job. To survive you had better be prepared to fight, even when the odds didn't look as if they were in your favor. His private line rang. Only a handful of trusted people had this number, and that's the way he wanted it. "Jacob here," said the proud investigator.

"What's on your mind, Lieutenant? More corpses to be identified, I suppose or is this a social call?" Jacob asked.

"It's both business and social, Jacob," came the answer from Bill Jones. The two friends always jested with one another. Their working relationship had been built on solid grounds, and unless the skies fell down, it would stay that way. "I was coming up your way and wondered if you would have time to have coffee with me. You know, our favorite place just down the street from your office. Could meet you there in twenty minutes?" the homicide detective concluded.

Jacob had the feeling the Lieutenant was up to something. The tone of his voice was different. Like someone who is anxious, to tell you what he is not supposed to. He would soon find out.

Both Anne and Laura were in the office, and on his way out, he told them where he was going to meet with the head of homicide.

"Well, Jacob, I do have some news for you. Joey Durango was found dead in his cell this morning. Another inmate on the same cellblock had stabbed him twenty one times in the chest. It looks like Profacini is beginning to feel the heat from different sources. There had been a rumor circulating around the county jail that Mr. Durango, in order to save his skin, was going to become crown witness in the counterfeit case. Again according to 'a reliable informer,' kid Joey was going to point the finger at Vito Profacini. This won't happen now. I hear the Feds are quite disturbed about losing their potential star witness. Furthermore, they have launched an internal investigation hopefully to find who leaked the information about Durango."

"You don't think it could be one of the FBI agents who did it for money? Myself I think one of the guards who overheard the conversations is most likely the person who would sell this kind of information. Maybe they should keep an eye on the staff from that section of the jail and see who makes a substantial purchase, like a new car for cash, in the next little while," said the private eye. "The more I think about it, Lieutenant, the more I tend to believe that Vito is already in possession of a large amount of counterfeit money. Now that Durango is out of the way, we will begin seeing these bills popping up all over the place. My sting operation should be put in high gear immediately, don't you think so Lieutenant?"

Bill Jones was slowly sipping his coffee thinking about the situation. Would it help solve a murder or two? If that were the case, the homicide man would definitely be willing to put the pressure on. No need to get an okay from the Captain if the results are successful for the LAPD. There was the danger of having any of the officers involved killed or maimed. If that happened, he would be in deep trouble with his Captain and the Police Commissioner. Still, he thought, if we don't do anything about this situation, it will keep on going and more people will be eliminated from the surface of this earth. It took a couple of calls from Jacob to bring him out of his concentration. "Sorry, Jacob, I was trying to look at the consequences if we did go ahead, and if we didn't. Right now, it doesn't look good. I think a meeting with Special Agent Ryle is in order, and the sooner the better."

"You're right, Lieutenant. I'll call Ryle this morning and maybe the three of us can get together for a quick meeting over lunch. I can't keep Lily on the hook forever, and without her our sting operation is down the drain."

Anne was positive she had located the source of Longhaul's equipment problems. Vandalism towards a large company is usually caused for an extortion purpose. In the case of Graham Longhaul his problem was closer to home. She had located a former employee who had been fired some eight months back. From interviews with other drivers who had said the guy was at times erratic in his behavior, she found out the man had made threats to the majority of drivers when he left, warning them to watch their driving. Larry Treeholder, a Native American, had been kicked off his own reservation because of his behavior towards others. At work, his frequent bouts of drunkenness had convinced management to let him go. Larry was a chronic drinker they had said. Because of the equipment he had to handle in his workday, he had become a high risk for accidents. The company feared it would have problems with its insurance carrier if it were found that an accident happened because an employee drank on the job. The decision had been unanimous and termination was immediate.

According to several staff members Anne had interviewed, Treeholder had made direct threats to some drivers. He knew the routes they were taking and the content of the cargo. So far, the vandalism had not caused a death, but it was only a question of time before it did. All the evidence the female gumshoe had gathered pointed directly to Larry Treeholder. After taking over the case from Jacob and because the vandalism had crossed state lines, it was decided she would consult with the FBI. A meeting was arranged with special agent Don Ryle's office. Anne brought over all of the evidence she had on file including the location where Treeholder was living, Silver City, New Mexico. Finding him had been easy. The company had sent his last paycheck to his former address in Texas and the post office forwarded his mail to Silver City. A paper trail can be a very reliable source when one wants to locate a person. Mr. Treeholder wanted to make sure he received all the money due him from his former employer, thus the reasons for a forwarding address.

Anne was going to wait until Larry Treeholder was arrested by the FBI and charged with vandalism endangering public safety before notifying the owner of the company, Graham Longhaul. She didn't have to wait too long. Within three days Treeholder was arrested and brought in front of a Federal judge. A trial date was penciled on the calendar and because the vandalism was one of high potential risk to the general public, bail was set at half a million dollars. Since the accused could not come forward with the bail, he was remanded in Federal custody until the trial date.

Jacob had been happy with the work Anne did as a secretary and even more pleased with her work as a private investigator. She was thorough, meticulous and wrote down every detail that came to mind whether she thought they were pertinent to the case or not. The work at the agency had grown tremendously. The gumshoe was proud of his partner and never hesitated to discuss his own cases with her or turn any file over if he felt her way of doing things would solve the problem faster. They were a good working match and since Laura handled the office work to perfection or just about to perfection, Jacob was able to concentrate better on his own cases.

He had received a call from George Murdoch who was concerned his brother's murder was not being solved. Mr. Murdoch was worried about the length of time it was taking to find, as far as he was concerned, the person who killed his brother at the back door of a bar. The place, he said, was filled with people every night. Didn't anyone see someone follow Carl out the back door or hear the gun shot? He had said to Jacob. As much as he could, the gumshoe had tried to reassure George Murdoch that he was still working on the case and would soon come to a positive identification of the murderer. The private eye could not give away all the information he had on file. He certainly could not let an outsider to law enforcement be privy to inside information concerning a sting operation or anything of relevancy to the case. He understood Murdoch's frustrations not to mention some of his own.

Still, Jacob tried to be as compassionate as possible. *That is all part of the job,* he thought. The work of a Law Enforcement practitioner whether in a civil servant situation such as being a member of a Police force or a private investigator could be very demanding at times, especially with family members of a murdered victim. An investigation never moved fast enough. People wanted these crimes solved immediately. The demanding public frowned upon any delay. If a case was not solved right away, accusations of incompetence or cover-up were the first words to make the headlines in local dailies. *Now, Jacob thought, what can I do to speed up the process and stay within the legal limits of the law?* These thoughts were going through his mind when Laura knocked on his door. "Come on in," he said.

"I have a couple of messages here for you, Mr. Schreiber, nothing of an urgent nature. Oh! There is a message from a Mrs. Marlene Bay, a former client I understand, she would like you to return her call at your convenience. If it's okay with you, I would like to leave early today. It's my son's birthday and we planned a little party for him. He's going to be nine."

"You may leave now if you wish, Laura, and lock the front door when you do. By the way, here's a ten-dollar gift for your son. Did you not tell me his name is William? Does he like baseball? I could have him on my little league team if he would like to play, Jacob said.

"I'll have to ask him. I know he likes basketball, but baseball I'm not so sure about. William is more of an intellectual than a sports kid. He likes to read a lot. I'll let you know tomorrow. That's very nice of you to ask and thank you for the money gift. I'm sure he'll pocket it and put it to good use."

After Laura had gone, Jacob looked at the telephone messages she had left with him. The name Juan Arturo stuck in his mind. Where had he seen or heard the name before? Then it struck him. There had been a guy by the name of Miguel Arturo who was gunned down gangland style in front of a restaurant which had a big sign with the name of the restaurant on it; JUAN ARTURO. The place was downtown Los Angeles near the railway station. He dialed the telephone number curious as to what Mr. Arturo would want from him. When someone answered the telephone he identified himself and asked to speak to Juan Arturo. "Jacob Schreiber here, Mr. Arturo. What can I do for you?" said the gumshoe.

"Mr. Schreiber, I have a big problem and would like for you to help me with it. The police don't care because I'm Mexican, and because my brother was killed just outside my door last year. They said he was part of a gang dealing in drugs. They think I deal in drugs too, but I don't. I am an honest businessperson and work hard to make my living. Could I come to see you or maybe you come taste the best Mexican food in Los Angeles at my restaurant and I'll tell you what my big problem is," said a worried sounding restaurant owner.

"I'll take you up on your offer, Mr. Arturo, and come down to see you around five o'clock," Jacob said. He wondered what the problem could be. Did it have to do with the LAPD or was it someone else? Next call to make was to Marlene Bay. He thought she might want an update on his investigation involving the Red Dahlia. *Well, there's only one way to find out,* as he dialed her number.

## CHAPTER TWENTY ONE...

Special Agent Don Ryle of the FBI was concerned that a crown witness had been eliminated gangland style. The Profacini group showed no respect for law enforcement people or individuals associated with law enforcement agencies whether male or female. Their style was a reminder of a not so long ago Chicago gangster by the name of Al Capone. Ryle wanted to put a stop to Mafia activities in Southern California. He knew the only way to succeed would be to convict the godfather himself to a long-term jail sentence. *Easier said than done*, he thought. Profacini had the best of criminal lawyers available to himself. Not a day went by when the G-man tried to come up with facts that would help convict the gangster in Federal court. Then one day a thought occurred to him. What if he could find someone he trusted enough to confide to? That someone would be willing to set up a trap in which Profacini would fall. It would have to be set in such a way that the masterminded criminal Vito was would not detect it. Then it hit him. "Of course," he said aloud, "there is such a person." Who else but Jacob Schreiber could make a sting operation work to the benefit of law enforcement. Now, that was history since the private eye had already approached him on the subject. He had agreed to assign two of his men and one woman to the scheme. Nothing had happened in the past ten days. His threesome had not reported anything of a positive nature. In fact, they had mentioned that the sting operation appeared to be going nowhere at the moment. Special Agent Ryle was thinking about the situation and wondering if a telephone call to Jacob Schreiber would be the right thing to do at this time. A knock on his door startled him and he automatically said, "Come in."

His secretary informed him that Mr. Schreiber was here and would like to see him. "Bring Jacob right in, please," said a surprised FBI agent.

"Sorry I didn't call before coming over but I figured we would have to get together anyway. This is rather urgent. Lily was at my office this morning. You look surprised. She's the woman I chose to do the sting at the Red Dahlia. The big goon she's been working on told her late last night that something big is going down tonight at the Red Dahlia. She told me this Carlo guy said for her not to be at the bar tonight. He told her Vito Profacini himself would be there to make sure the transfer of items. Yes, that's what he said, items would go smooth. Angelo Perilli, a godfather from back east was coming to town. The meeting is to go on at ten tonight. Lilly said she overheard him talk to one of his sidekicks about bringing a suitcase full of play-money to be turned over to the Perilli boys."

Before Jacob could go on further Ryle offered him coffee. What the special agent wanted was a break in the conversation to analyze what he had just heard.

"You know, Jacob, this sounds like the cows are returning to the barn. We better plan an immediate strategy and involve Lieutenant Jones in it," said the Special Agent. "Let me call him right now, he could come here to meet us both, I imagine."

The three friends talked for an hour over coffee and doughnuts. Their strategy was simple. Surround the club and block all escape routes. With a couple of decoys inside as well as outside to inform on new arrivals, the plan would require some twenty offic-ers. Ten would be from the LAPD narcotics and fraud division, and ten from the FBI Los Angeles Office. They figured about four to five cars maximum would arrive with the golden Mafia boys. Once the im-portant people walked out of the cars to go inside the bar, the idea was to subdue the drivers and side-kicks without alerting the inside crowd. This could be easy or disastrous depending on how fast the offic-ers would react.

Jacob told them that one of his informants had found out the Red Dahlia would be the meeting place because it was not owned by anyone associated with organized crime. The snitch said Vito knew about a few cops hanging around the place but was not concerned. In fact, he preferred the Red Dahlia instead of one of his own clubs. In a way, he had said, it would make the Detroit boys feel more comfortable. The informer did not think drugs were the items in question. One of the goons had mentioned cash, lots of it to be passed on for distribution in the Midwest and the East Coast.

"Now, if we can catch Vito red-handed here, we could end his operation," Jacob said.

It was a question of acting fast. Could the LAPD respond that quickly to a 'maybe it will happen' situation? Would there be too many questions to answer from the governing body? The Lieutenant seemed confident that a plan such as this could be executed on a moment's notice. Trained officers did not need to know every detail of an operation to function quickly. Instinct was part of their daily routine. All agreed for the plan to be immediately activated.

The wheels were in motion and all that was required was a bit of luck on the law enforcement side. Whether it would happen the way they expected it or not, time would tell. Jacob had grilled Lilly and his informer to make certain this was not a set-up by the mob to make them look bad or trap the police in a deadly shootout. The three men agreed to meet two blocks away from the Red Dahlia at eight o'clock. This would give them plenty of time to position themselves without arising suspicion.

When Jacob arrived at his office, he had two urgent messages. One from Don Ryle and the second from Lieutenant Jones. He called Jones first and found out the action plan for that night had to be cancelled. The same on the FBI side. *Well,* he thought, *I'll snoop around on my own. Maybe something will come up.*

What he had found out from Juan Arturo the other night was still floating in his head. Maybe there was a connection between the harassment at Juan's restaurant and the murder of Carl Murdoch several miles away in West Los Angeles. Could it be there was a corrupt police officer who worked in downtown LA, but lived in West LA, and is involved in the counterfeit scheme? If this was the case, he understood why the Mafia boys knew when undercover officers would be working the Red Dahlia. The information had to come from inside the police circle and be given by someone who played a dual role, someone who was taking dirty money without fear of being found out. This was a delicate subject to talk about with his friend Lieutenant Jones. Somehow, he would have to approach it whether Jones liked it or not.

Police forces were not very good when it came to investigating one of their own. Their first instinct was to cover up as much as possible for the 'good name of the force' they would say. Wow! What a mess this whole situation was becoming. Here he thought he could quickly nail who had killed Carl Murdoch. The more he dug into it, the more he felt he was at a dead-end. Not a good situation for a private investigator to find himself in. This rather made him question his techniques and abilities. So far, no one else seemed to think that way. Then a thought occurred to him. Why not involve Anne in this investigation? She was a new face with a different approach that could possibly find different answers than he had so far.

He walked to Laura's desk and said he would like to see Anne when she came in. No sooner had he said it that in came one of the rare and best female private eye in Southern California. "When you have a moment, Anne, could you come talk with me for a while. I have some thoughts I would like to throw your way," Jacob said.

After he spoke frankly, Anne helped him put a plan together that might bring better results than he'd had so far. Her first assignment would be to take her husband to dinner at Juan Arturo's place. No one in the LAPD, except for Lieutenant Jones knew who she was. Jones did not frequent Mexican restaurants. She could observe without fear of having a finger pointed in her direction. Her husband did not have to know she was on a work mission. This way no personal questions would be asked. She would make up an excuse about the need for the two of them to celebrate her becoming a partner since she had been too busy to do so earlier.

That same night Anne and her husband Bill enjoyed a wonderful Mexican dinner. All the time they were in the restaurant, Anne kept her eyes on who was there and who came in and out. At one point, she noticed a man in his mid-thirties walk in fast and immediately go to where the entrance to the kitchen was. He wasn't dressed like a police officer but his pants and shoes gave him away. She excused herself and got up to walk towards the ladies room which happened to be in the same direction as the kitchen. Instead of going to her left she walked through the kitchen doors and looked surprised when she saw the man in an argument with Juan Arturo. "None of my business," she said, "but this is an unusual place to find the ladies' room." The young man dashed out and as he did so mumbled something incoherent to Anne.

"Just before you came through the doors you should have turned left, lady," said a nervous restaurant owner.

Anne decided immediately to identify herself to Juan Arturo. It seems to calm him down knowing someone working with Mr. Schreiber would be here to protect him. After noting the information he had given her, she returned to her table. Bill had not even noticed where she had gone. As they walked out of the restaurant, Anne noticed a police car parked immediately in front of her car. She made a mental note of the car number for future reference. With the information the owner had given her, she had enough to begin a watch on what could very well be a crooked cop. Tomorrow was another day and a restful night was in order. As they passed the parked police cruiser, she noticed the two officers inside were in a heated argument. Something was going on and it appeared that one of the partners did not like it.

At the morning briefing with Jacob, she related the information given to her by Juan Arturo. She also mentioned her observations regarding the police officer that had rushed into the restaurant without his cap and what appeared to be an argument in the kitchen. Jacob thanked her for helping out. He informed her on his observations at the Red Dahlia. The two famous dons did not show up as they were scheduled to. Instead some goon from back east got drunk and wanted to start a fight with anybody. One of the Profacini boys convinced him to quietly leave with him. Nothing out of the ordinary and that bothered Jacob. He was beginning to feel the frustration creeping up on him. He knew the meeting place had been changed at the last minute. How could Vito have known about his plan of action? Impossible, just a coincidence or was it?

Too many ifs were popping up. Something somewhere was not right. Could it be that the leaks of information came from a higher source? Anne made the suggestion that he should have a face to face talk with the Lieutenant and lay out his apprehensions. Jacob picked up the telephone and dialed Bill Jones private number. "Jacob here, Lieutenant. Could you meet me for lunch at the Wilshire Country Club?" the gumshoe asked. "Yes, it's important or I would not take you away to a deserted place," he concluded with a jesting sound in his voice. Now he had to think on how to approach this problem. He had always been direct and truthful with his friend from Homicide. This time it was not different, that's the approach he would take.

"Well, Jacob, what is so important and urgent that you have to bribe me with lunch at one of the most exclusive places in LA?" commented the Lieutenant with a smile on his face. "Really what can I do for you this time that I haven't been able to do before?"

"We may be able to help each other out in this situation. You're going to jump right up when I tell you what I think is going on. What I really want you to do, if you can, both as a damn good homicide investigator and as a friend, is listen well to all I have to say. Yes, it's that serious. Let me rephrase that, it could become that serious." Jacob went on to explain his theory on the possibilities of two crooked cops knowing their every move. One at the top and one from the ranks. "They may not be working together, but they could be," Jacob continued.

Forty-five minutes later the look on the Lieutenant's face told it all. Jacob could see that he was hurt.

"You are giving me grounds to get myself suspended here," said a worried Lieutenant. "We're going, at least I am going to tread very delicately about this situation. I'll need some time on this Jacob. I just cannot barge into the Captain's office and announce we have a crooked cop in the force and a crooked commissioner to go along with it. This is something I have suspected for a long time, but I have been too busy to think about it. I need proof that will stand up to the toughest of scrutiny. This is not going to happen overnight, Jacob. I'll need a few days to get my thoughts together. In the meantime, you are going to have to hold the lid on the patrol officer working the downtown beat. Let's get back together on this subject three days from now. Is that agreeable with you my friend?"

"It is, Lieutenant. Please call on me if you need my assistance. For you I'm available twenty four hours a day," said the private eye. As Jacob left the club's parking lot, he knew his friend was disappointed. For a career and honest police officer there is nothing more disturbing than finding out about a crooked member of the force. The doubts it creates with the public take a long time to fade away. Still the bitterness and personal hurt lingers on for a long time.

## CHAPTER TWENTY TWO

The surprised look on Jacob's face was a thing to see. He had been nominated for a citizen award by the Los Angeles City Council for his contribution to law and order as a private person. He was to be the first recipient of the new implemented awards program the City of Angels was putting out. No one else was nominated. Jacob believed his friend Lieutenant Jones had placed his name forward. He was surprised again when he found out Jack Fundalee, the DA, was the one behind his nomination. For some time now, the City fathers had wanted to generate a positive image to bring back people who had left following the closing of the war industry supplies. New companies were establishing themselves and job opportunities were on the rise. Any publicity showing that crime was on the decline would create a better image and incite people to move where the jobs were. The economy was growing at a fast pace and people were needed.

Jacob was quietly reading over the hand delivered letter he had received from the City Council when Anne came in. "You won't believe what I have just received," he said to his partner as he handed the letter for her to read.

"This is great, Jacob. You certainly have done your part as a private citizen to help clean up the crime situation. I just came back from Juan Arturo's restaurant and found out Mr. Arturo is in the hospital. He was assaulted last night at closing time. The busboy I talked to was very upset. He told me it was a police officer who beat up on his boss. They're all afraid to talk about it. Everyone fears reprisals from the police. I think we should make a fast move on this situation. If we don't, more people are going to be hurt, if not killed, by this greedy and corrupted cop. This is not an easy case to handle but I suggest you pay a visit to Juan Arturo in the hospital," Anne concluded.

"Well," Jacob said. "The rats are coming out of their holes and it's time for the exterminator to do his job. I'm going to pay a visit to Mr. Arturo with Lieutenant Jones in tow. Maybe he will give us the name of the patrol officer who did this to him," Jacob concluded.

"You had better not introduce the Lieutenant to our Mexican client, as a police officer. They all have the same fear when it comes to law enforcement. If I was you I would think about that," Anne said.

Jacob realized his partner was right as he left for police headquarters. Bill Jones was surprised to see him there but agreed to go with him to the hospital. Once on their way the Lieutenant found out about Juan Arturo and the beating he had received at the hands of a police officer.

"Do you think he'll tell us who did it, Jacob. The majority of witnesses never want to testify openly as they fear reprisals worse than the original damage. You can introduce me as an associate since this man does not know who I am, and may not want to talk freely if he does," Bill Jones said.

When they came out of the hospital, both Jacob and the Lieutenant were not too happy with the situation. Jones was upset that an officer, who is supposed to protect and serve, turns out to be as bad as the goons who work for Profacini are. The name of the officer and his badge number would be easy to check. Now, if what Anne had said about the two partners arguing in the car turned out to be a fact, it could be the edge needed to rid the police force of this individual. Again, this was easier said than done. The Lieutenant insisted that Jacob come with him to headquarters when he checked the roster of the force to find a photograph of this officer.

"Look at these photos, Jacob, out of Police Academy training. Here's our man. Now I know why his name sounded so familiar to me. He's the nephew of our Commissioner. Maybe we've hit the jackpot here, my friend," Bill Jones said. "If we really want to catch this guy, we're going to have to trap him. Do you have any suggestions?" the Lieutenant asked.

"Well, I do, Lieutenant. Remember what Juan Arturo told us about the officer wanting $200 a week for protection. Let's plant some marked bills easily identifiable. You're going to need someone's cooperation from the inside. Anyone you can trust with this kind of game?" Jacob asked.

The Lieutenant thought for a moment, then said; "Yeah I think Captain Tom Harris would be the right person. Let me go see if he's in." A few minutes passed and the Lieutenant returned to ask Jacob to follow him.

"Captain Harris, this is Jacob Schreiber," as the Lieutenant introduced the gumshoe. The two looked at each other and smiled.

"I remember you, Schreiber, you're the guy who pulled me out of the water when our boat was hit by a Japanese torpedo. I'm really happy to see you again. I have heard so much about you from the Lieutenant here and other members of the force, I thought you were part of the LAPD. I understand you have something of a very sensitive nature to tell me. I'm all ears," said the Captain.

Jacob went on to relate his story beginning with the first telephone call he had received from Juan Arturo. Forty minutes later Captain Harris just shook his head in disbelief.

"The Lieutenant has strong credibility in this department and so do you, Jacob Schreiber. Because of that I have no hesitation to believe what you have just told me. I'm going to arrange for a change of partner tonight and see what's going to happen. Don't let that stop you from marking the bills like you suggested. If we could only find something to get rid of the present commissioner, I would be the happiest man on the LAPD roster," concluded the Captain.

After another fifteen minutes of reminiscing war stories, Jones and his gumshoe friend left the Captain's office. "Let's put the wheels in motion," Jacob said. "We'll use the ten bills the Captain gave us, since he jotted down the serial numbers. This way we can't miss, Lieutenant, and let's hope we can prevent snoopy reporters from finding out about it until it hits the courts."

Juan Arturo did not take any convalescent time. He returned to work the moment he came out of the hospital. He could not let Jacob Schreiber down. Juan carried in his pockets the ten marked bills Jacob had handed over to him. For extra security, Jacob had convinced the restaurant owner to let him wash the dishes so he could have an eye on the transaction between Juan and Julian Post, a crook in uniform, but not for long. They didn't have to wait too long. At about ten o'clock the patrol officer walked into the kitchen looking for Juan. Jacob, from behind the dishwashing counter, watched the transaction take place. His favorite photographer was hiding in a tall closet where he was able to see the whole kitchen scene and take pictures at will. The only comment made by the patrol officer was; "See you next week, wetback."

"Well, Juan, you did it without fear and, trust me, that's the way it's going to be from now on. As we speak, this crooked cop is being handcuffed, arrested and thrown in jail. You will not have this problem anymore," Jacob said.

"Without you, Mr. Schreiber, I don't know what I would have done. I was so scared when that man came in my kitchen, I thought my hands were shaking. Then I saw you standing there and felt protected. Thank you and tell the police Captain I will testify if he wants me to," said a relieved restaurateur.

The next morning Jacob received a personal telephone call from Captain Harris who informed him that Julian Post had been charged with extortion and assault with a deadly weapon.

*If only it was as easy to pin down Carl Murdoch's killer,* the gumshoe thought. He figured he would have to spend more time at the Red Dahlia. Maybe intensify the sting operation or find a way to trap Vito Profacini.

Laura opened his office door to let Lieutenant Jones in, who was carrying coffee and doughnuts. "I was just about to call you, Bill. Your Captain Harris already called to bring me up to date on Julian Post. This is not the end of the crooked cop case, my friend. I wonder how many other small businesses he terrorized. His regular partner must know something. Anyway, I'm sure the Captain is on top of things. I certainly owe you one for doing what you did for me. I know, it's all part of a day's work, but just the same, without you I would have had to use stronger tactics. Thanks again, Lieutenant. Let's have this coffee and a doughnut you were kind enough to bring in. I am still trying to put together a plan to get to Vito. There has to be a weakness somewhere in his façade. The difficult part is to find it," the private eye said.

"It may not be as hard as you think, Jacob. I know from a good source that this Mafioso likes to gamble. I'm not talking blackjack but high-stake poker games. A source of mine told me that he and some special invited guests get together once a month at a designated location right here in Los Angeles. I have also been informed that our commissioner has been seen in Profacini's company on a regular monthly basis. Now, if we could catch these two birds at the same time we would do society a great service. Commissioner Zachary Millen was never a favorite of mine. From the beginning when he was appointed I always had the feeling this guy was not always kosher. It's just a gut feeling you know. I have not been wrong too often in my assessment of human behavior. Those psychology courses I took at university have paid off over the years," Lieutenant Jones concluded.

"I know what you mean my friend. I didn't take psychology but I have the same gut feeling as you do," Jacob said. "I could place a tail on the commissioner without his knowledge. This way we could possibly find out where he meets with his Mafia friends for high-stake poker. If you get me profiles of him and his nephew, I'll dig further in their backgrounds. We may get lucky and find something no one around here knows about. Before our former Mayor  appointed this man, did anybody know anything about him? Where does he come from anyway? You think you could get me a fact sheet on the two? Not that I need it, but it would speed up the search.

"Just make sure you don't do anything to cause any suspicion around you," Jacob concluded.

"There's no danger of that, my friend. My secretary can dig it out in a moment. It would be interesting to find out if what he officially stated as his background matches what you will find. Good thinking, Jacob, I'll get it over to you later today," Bill Jones said as he got up to leave.

Jacob immediately called a friend who was good at tailing people, and who happened to be a good photographer at the same time. The fact that he worked for a major newspaper was a plus. Harvey Moon had been a sidekick of Jacob's all through the war and the two had remained friends ever since. The gumshoe knew he could depend on this man's discretion until the time came to expose the culprit. Again this was not directly involved with finding who killed the piano player but one never knows in which direction a little digging will take him.

The ring of his telephone startled him. "Jacob Schreiber here. I see, why don't you come by my office now if you can. Four o'clock will be fine, make sure you bring the big envelope you just mentioned," Jacob concluded before putting the telephone down.

*I wonder what this is all about,* he thought. *Why would a crooked cop's wife want to give me evidence that would jeopardize her husband's chances of a lesser sentence?*

*Interesting, but I had better call Lieutenant Jones to be here with me.*

## CHAPTER TWENTY THREE

Paula Post arrived at Jacob's office looking like a woman who had just run the mile in record time. Her face was flushed and she had dark circles under her eyes. She couldn't have been more than 35 but in her state of mind, she looked much older. She carried a small briefcase and held it tight on her lap as she waited to see Jacob Schreiber. He, on the other hand, was not comfortable about talking privately with the wife of a crooked cop just about ready to go to trial. Lieutenant Jones had accepted Jacob's invitation to be present after consulting with the DA's office. Laura, on instructions from Jacob, had made Mrs. Post sit in the waiting area and offered her a coffee, which she refused. She just sat there nervously as if time was not passing by fast enough. At the given time Laura knocked on Jacob's door and announced that Paula Post was here. She was informed to bring her right in.

"Have a seat, Mrs. Post," Jacob said. "This is Lieutenant Jones head of Homicide at the LAPD. Do you have any objections to his taking part in our meeting?" the gumshoe asked. The woman shook her head negatively.

She opened the briefcase and pulled out several envelopes, which she placed in front of Jacob. "In there you will find enough to put Julian and his uncle behind bars for a very long time I hope," said a distraught woman. "The last three years have been extremely difficult for me. You see, Mr. Schreiber, I have no family close by to whom I could confide. My husband, I'm sad to say, was and is a tyrant, a womanizer and a goon. The people he is supposed to protect he has been terrorizing for years. He has some direct contact with a Mafia guy by the name of Profaci, Profici ...I can't remember, but I know his first name is Vito."

"Vito Profacini it is, Mrs. Post" Jacob interjected.

"He informed this Vito about upcoming raids on his nightclubs and many times I heard your name mentioned in a way one would wish you dead. We have no children and thank God for that. I planned to move out of the house shortly and not let him know where I am going. You see, Mr. Schreiber, I'm afraid of him. I know he would kill me if I gave him a reason to. In several of his telephone conversations, I heard him tell this Mafia guy not to worry anymore about so and so. Within a day or two after such a conversation, he would make a substantial bank deposit, take me out to dinner and spend money like there's no tomorrow. I figured something was going on, but I was afraid to ask. At one point in a conversation with his uncle, you know, the police commissioner, I heard him talk about how good it was to have gotten rid of the piano player at the club in West LA. In the last six months, I noted the telephone calls he made and received at home. It's all in one of the envelopes I gave you. You will also find in there some information that shows who Zachary Millen really is. Don't look so surprised, he's the best con man to come along in years," said a now smiling Paula.

"What you are giving me here, Mrs. Post, you should be giving to the DA himself. Would you mind if I call him while you're here? I know you can't testify against your husband but nothing can prevent you from doing so against the commissioner. Good, we'll just take a coffee break while I call Mr. Fundalee.

"Jacob Schreiber here, Mr. District Attorney. You already know that Mrs. Paula Post was going to visit me today? She's here now, and Lieutenant Jones is here. The evidence this lady just gave us is a bombshell, to say the least," Jacob said. "I think it would be better if we all came down to your office right now and turn this evidence over to you. Good, see you in a half hour, Jack."

"The DA has opened the door to offer you protection, Mrs. Post. He did say that you would not have to testify in court against your husband, but would like a statement from you. You're moving your head 'yes,' do I understand you are ready to come to the DA's office now?" Jacob said.

"I am, Mr. Schreiber. Extortion will not be enough to put those two awful people away for a long enough time. I had two years of law studies before I met with 'prince charming'. It took me a year to pierce through his armor. Since then, I have been afraid to say anything to him in reference to money, his uncle or his work. There is a list in one of the envelopes, which shows names of people and names of businesses with sums of money next to them. I did not make up the list, it's in his own handwriting. For some reason, he has been having a difficult time to post bail. You see, Mr. Schreiber, the house is in my name and so is the bank account. I know he has another bank account somewhere with serious cash in it, but I don't know where and have not been able to find a bankbook. Maybe he kept it in his locker at work, afraid I may find out what he was hiding. Enough chitchat, I'm ready to go now," said a nervous Paula. "May I ride with you? I'm just too nervous to drive right now."

The three of them got in Jacob's new car. A few days ago, he had just purchased a new Cadillac fresh from the factory. Ten minutes later they all walked in Jack Fundalee's office. After Paula was introduced, they all tried to sit quietly while the DA looked at the contents of the two envelopes and questioned Mrs. Post about it.

"You're going to need some police protection, my dear lady. I'll let the Lieutenant handle that. I'm sure he can find some trusted men to protect you from your husband and his famous uncle. Do you think you could arrange to leave town for a while? At least until the trial begins. This way neither Julian Post nor the commissioner would be able to get to you. This is very serious, Mrs. Post. Knowing how Profacini reacts, he could easily arrange that you have an accident and not survive it. Know what I mean?" said a concerned District Attorney.

"If Julian—or should I say when—Julian finds out I'm the one responsible for the information you have, Mr. Fundalee, I'm as good as six feet under. His uncle's real name is not Millen, but I don't know what it is. I heard Julian call him Skip many a time. My god! Why did somebody not think of checking his fingerprints with the FBI? That would certainly clear some of the mystery around the man," Paula Post said.

Lieutenant Jones said; "When he officially became commissioner the LAPD had to supply him with a photo ID. I remember when they took his fingerprints he made a joke as if 'You've got me now, I surrender,' and everyone had a good laugh. I'll get a copy of his prints and ask our friend Special Agent Ryle to check them out on their national files. I'm going to get them and move fast on this one. We don't have much time to spare. However good of a con man he is, time is running out on his little gig."

"Let's go back to my office, Lieutenant, so you can get your car. Before we leave, could you arrange to have protection for Mrs. Post? Your men should be instructed the protection order includes both her husband and the commissioner. Neither one should have access to her," the gumshoe concluded.

The DA thanked everyone for their cooperation and assured them he would immediately put the wheels of justice in high gear.

When Jacob found himself alone in his office, he tried to place everything in the proper order. He took a large drawing pad with which he always liked to work and began writing a sequence of events beginning with the call he had received from the Lieutenant about his business card being found in a victim's pocket. By the time he got to Paula Post, almost three hours had gone by. He still didn't know who had actually killed Carl Murdoch. More importantly, who had given the order to eliminate the piano player and why! In his process of elimination, the wrong answers surfaced. At least this is what he thought. What if they were the right answers? *All I have to do is come up with the proof,* he thought. Jacob kept pointing arrows, drawing lines from one scene to the other and nothing definite came up. Was it that obvious that he could not see it? There were three sleepers in this case, more than one usually has in a simple murder case. Still, Vito Profacini constantly popped up to the forefront. Was it because he was the number one suspect whenever someone got murdered gangland style? Did someone want to put the finger on Profacini for the murder of Carl Murdoch? Could it be that one of the sleepers did not want his name to surface in bad light anywhere? So many questions and not a positive answer to any of them. The more Jacob analyzed and thought, the more he was convinced someone had ordered the job other than Vito Profacini. The loud ringing of his telephone brought him back to the present.

"Schreiber here," he answered.

"Jacob, I've been trying to find you for the last half hour and then it dawned on me you could still be in the office. Just wanted you to know the new developments," the Lieutenant said. "Captain Harris was very helpful in finding the right men to keep an eye on Paula Post. Furthermore, he switched drivers on the commissioner. This may not sound like much but as you know, a driver hears a lot of confidential stuff. Julian Post succeeded to make bail through his lawyer and the guarantor, I found out, is no other than the commissioner. He went directly to his wife's residence and attempted to get in. Got in an argument and a fistfight with one of the officers. Was arrested again and this time the DA is making sure the bail will be too high for his uncle to guarantee."

"That's interesting, Lieutenant. Now if only I could pinpoint who murdered Carl Murdoch, I'd be in seventh heaven. Post can't be too smart to do what he did. The son of a bitch should be taken to a back alley and worked over for the pain he caused to poor old Juan Arturo. I'm sure the Captain will get a lot of witnesses for this case, but what about the commissioner's prints, anything new on that, Lieutenant?" Jacob asked.

There was a long silence on the telephone. It made Jacob wonder what was going on.

"Lieutenant," he almost shouted, "are you still there?" Jacob let out a sigh of relief when he could hear his friend talking to someone in the background.

"I'm here, Jacob. Here's some more good news about our 'too smart for his own good' commissioner. An FBI agent just handed me his five-sheet profile. Did you ever hear of a con artist who defrauded several banks along the East Coast and the Mid West about ten years ago? This happened before the war and the man was never caught. Although law enforcement people knew who he was, Patrick McCall-Post, better known by his nickname of Skip, had disappeared from the face of the earth. The photographs I have don't look like him, but fingerprints never lie. You're good at finding things, Jacob. Would you like to tag along with me when I pay a personal visit to Zachary Millen, better known as Patrick Post, brother of Julian Post's father?" said the head of homicide.

"This is the second best offer I've had today, Bill. Yes, I would like to tag along if it does not cause any internal problems for you," Jacob answered. "Do you want me to come to your office? Oh, I see, you're giving me the red carpet treatment. What is all that going to cost me now?" Jacob jested. "I'll be ready when you get here, Lieutenant. This should be one of the most enjoyable encounters I have had in a long time," the gumshoe concluded before putting the telephone down.

No sooner had he done so, it rang again. "Schreiber here, can I help you with something?" he said. Jacob was surprised to hear the voice of Rodney Spikes, manager of the Red Dahlia, inviting him over for a drink and some interesting information on a conversation he had overheard early on. Jacob told him he would certainly come by, but did not know at which time yet. As he was waiting for the Lieutenant to pick him up he could not help but wonder what Rodney Spikes had heard that was so important for him to call. The more he thought about it, the more he convinced himself to go to the Red Dahlia and let the Lieutenant handle the commissioner. When the homicide detective showed up, they had a short conversation and Jacob went directly to his car on his way to West LA.

## CHAPTER TWENTY FOUR

Jacob arrived at the Red Dahlia as the musicians were stepping off stage. He noticed the man walking away from the piano was not Tim Huckles. The gumshoe went directly to the bar, ordered a beer and asked the barman if Rodney Spikes was in. In less than two minutes the manager showed up and invited the private eye to a corner table away from the crowd and the performing stage. The place was not as full as he had seen it on other occasions. Jacob did notice the Profacini boys glittered by their absence. Maybe they and Huckles were holding a meeting somewhere.

"I'm glad you came over, Mr. Schreiber. Mrs. Bay told me on several occasions I should not hesitate to contact you if something out of the ordinary bothered me. Well, something is disturbing me to say the least. Let me see where I can begin," Rodney Spikes said.

"Just take your time and tell it to me as you go along. I'm good at figuring puzzles. So whatever it is, please don't think it may not be important, just throw it in the conversation. I'll stop you if you get off track. By the way, I hope this concerns the murder of Carl Murdoch. And please call me Jacob," the gumshoe concluded.

"That it does, Jacob," said the bar manager. "Earlier tonight some big guy who has been coming here on a regular basis came in and motioned to Tim Huckles to join him. What I heard this goon say is almost unreal. I don't know if you are aware of this but according to these two guys, the LA police commissioner is in bed with the Mafia. He is fattening his bank account with payoffs he gets from the Profacini family. I also heard there was a cop involved in the scheme but no names were given. The goon said the LAPD management was stupid. They don't know how many cops are on the take. Frank, I believe the goon's name is, told Huckles the police would never find out who ordered the killing of the former piano player. Although some of The Sons of God are still in jail he said, none of them knew all the details of the counterfeiting operation except for their deceased leader. This Mafia guy further said that when Vito was to meet with the Detroit godfather they had purposely leaked it to see what the LAPD was going to do. When Vito found out from his number one source, the commissioner, they changed the meeting place without anyone finding out where."

"Did Frank and Tim Huckles not know you could hear them talk?" Jacob asked.

"They couldn't have, Jacob. You see where that booth is on the other side of the stage the wall next to it is very thin. On the other side of that wall is a storage room where I keep cases of beers and liquor. I just happened to be in there when I heard Huckles talk. It caught my attention and I only stayed there for ten minutes max. When I came out Tim Huckles was using the telephone at the end of the bar and Frank was just leaving the place. No one paid attention to me as I was carrying some bottles to the bartender. I know you might think this was all staged by them to see if it would get to someone at the LAPD. Now that I know about the commissioner, it's not difficult to understand why the bad guys were always one step ahead of the police. I did hear Huckles say that Murdoch had to be eliminated. He only wished it could have been done further away from the club. There was no time to plan it he said, because they feared Murdoch was going to expose the whole counterfeiting plan that very night. That was the last thing I heard them talk about Jacob," the bar manager concluded.

"Where's Tim Huckles now?" Jacob asked.

"I don't know, Jacob, but twenty minutes after he put the telephone down this other piano player showed up and Tim left. He didn't say anything to me since his contract has a clause which allows him to get a replacement as long as he pays for it," Rodney Spikes concluded.

Jacob finished his beer and left the bar. He made sure no one was following him this time. He went straight home for a good night's rest, and to digest all the information this day had brought him.

The next morning he arrived at the office bright and early, but Anne and Laura had beaten him there. They were all excited about the latest news bulletin, and asked Jacob if he had heard about the arrest of the police commissioner by the FBI.

Apparently, they said his name was not Zachary Millen. He was a fugitive by the name of Patrick McCall-Post. The report said that he had changed his facial appearance through a series of medical procedures in South America. Patrick Post known by his nickname of Skip had disappeared after an audacious jailbreak some ten years ago. He was on the FBI most wanted list for defrauding several banks in the Boston and New York area for hundreds of thousands of dollars, possibly in the millions. No one knew the exact amount or at least pretended they didn't, the reporter had said. At the time the crime was committed there had been a couple of suicides amongst the elite of the banking world.

"Don't you think this is a fascinating story, Jacob," Anne said. "Besides, the FBI mentioned the help of private investigator Jacob Schreiber in solving a ten year old crime. The telephone has not stopped ringing since we walked in, Mr. Celebrity."

"It's all part of a day's work as far as I'm concerned. I wish it would be that easy to solve Carl

Murdoch's killing," said a smiling gumshoe. "If press people call for me, please tell them I am not available at the moment, but will return all calls later today."

As Jacob turned to walk towards his private office, the front door opened and in walked coffee and doughnuts being delivered by the Chief of Homicide himself. The ladies questioned the Lieutenant about the arrest since his name had also been mentioned in the news report. Bill Jones took a few minutes to satisfy their curiosity. Then he and Jacob had a great conversation where the Lieutenant filled in Jacob with the loose ends about the arrest of Patrick Post.

"Apparently, the Mayor  was upset that a con man was able to fool him and all of the LAPD while having access to the most sensitive police information available," Bill Jones said. " What the Mayor deemed to be upsetting about this 'commissioner' is that he had gained everyone's confidence and was in on all major confidential information concerning the activities of organized crime. He then transmitted key decisions and information data to the gangsters themselves," the detective said. "No wonder they were always a step ahead of us. Vito could afford to be friendly with us since his information came right from the top cop. The whole Police Department was made to look like incompetent nincompoops. Well, my friend, we put a stop to that last night. You should have seen his face when the FBI agent handcuffed him. He kept screaming that he would have their badges. Skip Post wanted to talk to his lawyer right now, he insisted. The four FBI agents just ignored him and took him away. He's on his way back to New York to face the charges he was supposed to have faced ten years ago, plus a few additional other ones, I would imagine. With this con man out of the way it may become easier to catch Profacini at something illegal without him knowing our every move ahead of time," said the Lieutenant.

"Let me tell you, Bill, I think I know who ordered the hit on Murdoch. I have a couple more things to verify then I'll give it all to you for the finale. A friend who has a business in Santa Monica told me a couple of days ago that some Italian guy tried to pass a phony $50 bill on him. He was just lucky, I guess. The bill looked too new and since he happened to have an old one in his wallet he compared the two and saw a discrepancy in the signature. The Italian guy snapped the bill from my friend and walked out of the store as fast as he could, not saying a word. The storeowner was able to catch the license plate of the car the man drove away in. Here it is, Lieutenant. Check it out and maybe this time you can do the FBI a favor," Jacob said.

As the Lieutenant left the office, Anne walked in for the regular weekly meeting. They discussed the many cases that were ongoing and what was to be done to close them. Jacob asked Anne to get involved in the Murdoch case with him again. He felt so close to a closure he could taste it. He just needed this final information to complete it.

"I would like you to check on these three guys, Tim Huckles, Jim Bates and David Storm. Here's a file on all three with their home addresses, photographs and other details you may or may not need. As you know they're the threesome who provide the music at the Red Dahlia. The FBI did not have anything on them. Maybe I'm barking up a wrong tree, but my gut feeling tells me I'm not. Huckles is the bandleader, and the one who seems to be on very friendly terms with the Profacini boys who hang around the bar. Question the neighbors, kids who play on the street near their residence. One never knows what may surface. I know you'll come up with something I haven't been able to put my finger on yet," Jacob concluded.

"I'll do my best, Jacob, and since no one knows me at the Red Dahlia I'll pull another one on my husband and invite him for a drink. This way I'll be able to see what these guys are up to. No need to worry, Jacob, I always have 'Millie' to protect me. She's well strapped to my back, but comes out quick when she's needed." Anne was talking about her hidden gun aside from the pea shooter .25 she carried in her purse.

Jacob just knew she would come up with additional information to help him conclude an overdue solution. He had to rush out of the office to meet one of his informers for lunch at the Hollywood Park. Larry had called him and said he had some information that could help him find Carl Murdoch's killer. *Now,* Jacob thought, *how could a guy who plays the ponies on a regular basis always pick up information on different crime scenes in the City?*

When he arrived at the track, he saw a few familiar faces including Vito Profacini himself who appeared to be on his way out. Jacob made sure the Mafioso did not see him. *No use to place my informant in danger when it's not necessary to do so, he thought.* As he walked into the restaurant, he saw Larry sitting by himself at a corner table. Greetings were short and Jacob ordered drinks for both. In his jacket pocket, he had an envelope with three hundred dollars if the information he was about to receive was important enough. They had lunch, laughed and talked about everything under the sun but the Murdoch case. After the coffee was served Larry suddenly pushed his chair back just enough so that he could lean on the table with his elbows. Jacob knew he was ready for a serious conversation.

"I was in a bar on Wilshire two nights ago, minding my own business, sipping a cold beer when I saw this big guy walk in. He's one of those rare out-of-size Mexicans, a little over six feet, around 230 lbs. and a mean face to go with the physique. He sat at the table next to mine, and within minutes, a smaller, well-dressed younger man joined him. The second guy I had seen with different Profacini boys over the months. I heard someone call him Frank one time. This guy has eyes of steel with an absolute blank look that would scare a grizzly away. I also heard from friends about this Frank guy, who warned me to stay away from him. They said his nickname is 'ice' as in pick. Therefore, I figured he's the guy who's responsible for two or three recent hits in this town. Then I heard the big Mexican ask him what he needed him for. 'Ice' was very direct in his response. He said; remember the guy who plays the piano at the Red Dahlia in West LA. Well Vito is afraid he may crack under pressure and sing like a canary. He doesn't know you, but if he sees me coming, he'll know something is up. I was supposed to eliminate that other piano player, but this Tim guy was in too much of a hurry. Someone else did the job. Nothing wrong with that, except for the location, just outside the back door of the bar. Yeah, Vito is afraid he would talk too much. They had a couple of more drinks and arranged to meet in two days to get the job done. That happens to be tomorrow Jacob," Larry concluded.

Jacob thanked him for his information, handed him the envelope from his inside left pocket and waited until he was out of sight before he got up himself. He thought the first thing to do was get Anne off the trail. The gumshoe rushed to his car and proceeded to his office. As he was rounding the parking lot exit, he noticed a car pulling out slowly. He himself slowed down and the car passed him. It was a young couple very much in a hurry to find a hiding place, he thought.

Back at the office, he called Lieutenant Jones for an urgent meeting. The two met before the end of the day and planned an immediate strategy. This time it would have to be done quickly without headquarters authorization. The Lieutenant would approach Tim Huckles before he got in his car and ask him to join him in the unmarked police car. If that didn't work, he would arrest him on the spot and take him to Jacob's office where the gumshoe would have a face to face talk with him. When the Lieutenant got to Huckles' street, he could see a commotion in front of him and lights flashing. A police car was already there. He was hoping that what he was thinking was not what had happened. Unfortunately it was. Tim Huckles had been gunned down just as he was to get in his car to drive down to the Red Dahlia. Bill Jones got out of his car and talked to the Sergeant who was controlling the crime scene. After spending twenty minutes there, he drove back to Jacob's office.

"How was your encounter with the piano player, Lieutenant?" Jacob asked.

"Didn't have one. Got there too late, the man was already dead. He had been shot four times at point blank range as he opened his car door. They got to him before we did, Jacob. Rotten luck we're having with this Red Dahlia," the homicide detective said.

"It may not be all that rotten after all, Lieutenant. Yesterday I had sent Anne Dombrowski on a wild goose chase after Huckles, Bates and Storm. The information she brought back is rather interesting. I always thought there was a sleeper in this case since Vito being the obvious choice was not the one who had done it. These musicians always have strong connections with drugs and organized crime. Our three musketeers are not different from the rest of them. Maybe I should have said our four musketeers to include Carl Murdoch," Jacob said.

"I don't know where you're going with these comments except to say that musicians are drug addicts and buy drugs from the mob," the Lieutenant questioned.

"No, to the generalization on drug addiction and a small yes, on dealing with the local godfather. You see, Lieutenant, most nightclubs belong to organized crime people. Except for the Red Dahlia which happens to be owned by a very nice old Los Angeles family. In order to be able to work, musicians have to put up with the boss's demands. Most of the time it's turning your head the other way when something unusual is going on. Unusual, that is, to the public. However, this was not the case here. It goes deeper than that. I don't know if I ever told you but Carl Murdoch had a son with a woman he never intended to marry. George Murdoch, brother of Carl, is raising the son. You look at me as if I'm telling you a story out of a church meeting. It's almost like that, Lieutenant. Let me get to the point. The woman who gave birth to Carl Murdoch's son was Patricia Bates, sister of Jim Bates. Now I see your eyebrows lifting. Yes, Patricia Bates died of an overdose of cocaine a year after her son was born. The cocaine had been given to her by Carl Murdoch who himself was addicted as we know. Jim Bates hated Murdoch for what he had done to his sister and had vowed revenge. Jim Bates is the guy who killed Carl Murdoch. Don't be surprised Lieutenant. My partner Anne found all this information when she began talking to the neighbors of Bates, Storm and Huckles. She ran into an ex girlfriend of Bates who got the whole story from him when he was feeling high. She signed a statement. Here it is, and she agreed to testify if we give her protection. You're the one with the protection capability, Lieutenant. Case closed, for the time being, wouldn't you say?" Jacob concluded with a grin from ear to ear.

The Lieutenant made two telephone calls before leaving Jacob's office. One was to have Jim Bates arrested for murder and the second to the DA's office.

As he placed his hand on the door handle, he turned around, looked at Jacob, smiled and told him, "Damn it, Schreiber, you're too good, you should be working with me. You and I would make one hell of a team. Southern California could turn into a paradise vacation place. No, from the look on your face you're not ready to become a nine-to-five cop."

~*~*~

About our Author
Guy Verreault (Pen Name Guy Beaulieu)

A former journalist, radio talk show host and hostage negotiator team member, Guy Verreault—pen name, Guy Beaulieu—is fluently bilingual in English and French. Although he writes fiction, many of his novels reflect incidents and experiences that occurred in the past. His narrative style complements the private eye dramas he writes. Reflective of heroic fictional private investigators of the ages—Mike Hammer, Spenser, Hercule Poirot, Shell Scott, Lew Archer, Travis McGee, and Philip Marlow, Verreault's action adventure stories are filled with unexpected twists and turns, romance, mystery and suspense as the good guy takes on all comers.

Guy Verreault
zephirin@shaw.ca

Other books in the *Jacob Schreiber Mystery* series

## THE DEATH OF A BOOKIE

### *Rave Reviews for The Death of a Bookie*

**"The Death of a Bookie"** by Guy Beaulieu is a fascinating book. From the moment the body of bookie Louis "The Snake" Billings, is found in the office of private investigator Jacob Schreiber, the reader is drawn into a story of intrigue and mystery.

### *Who killed the bookie?*

Was it his wife, Helen, who arranged the murder to avoid messy divorce proceedings? Or was it "Black Jack" Tony Padilla, a Mafia head, who ordered the hit because he'd caught the bookie skimming money from the 'family' operations? Apparently, someone is not happy to see Jacob investigating the case. So he finds his tires slashed with a threatening note attached. When this fails, several attempts on his life are made to scare him off.

But Jacob, an ex-marine, does not frighten easily.

And so he continues his investigation more determined than ever to solve the case.

Unfortunately, matters grow in complexity as more dead bodies keep popping up, and as he keeps digging Jacob uncovers a plot that threatens the security of the nation, itself.

Jacob is fortunate to have a strong liaison with Lieutenant Jones of the LAPD and Agent Trickten of the FBI. Will such connections help him when he comes face to face with the mob?

Can Jacob Schreiber rise to the challenge?

Read on to find out. The ending is sure to surprise you.

Guy Beaulieu's prose flows easily and his dialogue is natural and crisp.

The Death of a Bookie is a story that will delight, and I highly recommend it.

Mario Fedele
Author of God's Gift.

~*~*~

The Death of a Bookie
First in the Jacob Schreiber Mystery series
CHAPTER ONE...

**(September 1945)**

The morning sun was still peering through the smog on Hollywood Boulevard. Early morning brought two different species of society to life: the working class hurrying to get where they had to go, and the leftovers from the night before. Some, too drunk to go home, had slept on the sidewalk either directly in store entrances or close to them. The smell of vomit and urine was strong where the night warriors had fallen.

Six-thirty in the morning and Jacob was on his way to the office at Hollywood and Vine. Above the stench of the streets he could smell fresh brewing coffee. A good cup of coffee is all he wanted at this time of the day. He had an apartment on Sunset near Fairfax, and when the weather permitted, which was 95% of the time, he preferred walking to his office. As he approached the building, he could see several police cars. He wondered what could have happened. Probably someone was beaten to death. A police officer recognized Jacob and told him Lieutenant Jones was inside and would like to talk with him. Now Jacob's curiosity was piqued, and he ran up the two flights of stairs to his office. The old elevator was out of order.

From the landing, he could see the print on the glass door: "Jacob Schreiber Private Investigator, Divorces, Surveillance, You name it, I do it," in bold black with a trim of deep gold. He was proud of that sign. It had brought him many clients who really did not know what a P.I. was in 1945. As he approached the door, he could see the silhouette of men moving around inside. He wondered what the hell was going on here!

"There you are, Jacob," was the greeting he got from Los Angeles Police Lieutenant Bill Jones. "We got a call someone had been shot in this building early this morning. When the patrol officer got here and realized this was your office, he immediately put in a call for me. Your door had been left wide open, obviously the lock had been jimmied and the body could be seen from the hallway." The Lieutenant motioned Jacob to walk over to where the body was lying face down. The man had been shot in the back of the skull; blood was all over the place.

"The body was still warm when we got here, Jacob, so we figure the man was shot less than three hours ago, probably at about 4 AM. The coroner will try to confirm that." As he leaned down and turned the body over, he asked Jacob; "Do you know this guy?"

Jacob leaned forward and looked carefully at the man's shattered face. Yes, he did recognize the face but quickly debated if he should confirm that with the Lieutenant. "This is Louis-the-snake Billings as he was known. A bookie, loan shark, pimp, with many unmentionable undertakings only a low life individual like Louis would be involved in. His wife had hired me to tail him for divorce procedures about three months ago. He was not my client but I did meet him face to face once or twice. Why would somebody kill him in my office I wonder?"

Jacob proceeded to look around. If there was anything missing he couldn't detect it at first glance. Then he unlocked the heavy metal filing cabinet and started to go through it, drawer by drawer. He obviously could not immediately tell if any files were missing. Anne Dombrowski, his secretary, would be in later, around ten o'clock. She would be able to tell if something was missing.

"OK, Lieutenant, I can't see what he was doing here, but someone followed Louis here and did away with him. Since the divorce proceedings were coming up shortly, I can only imagine he was looking for the file I had on him. Do you know his wife's address? I have it here if you need it. Did you want me for anything else Lieutenant?"

"Not at this time, Jacob. Maybe in a day or two. Once I have more information on this character and the autopsy report, it might enlighten me. I'm going to have the coroner remove the body. The investigators are done with the picture taking and I imagine it would be useless to dust for prints. Just keep in touch with me in case you find something unusual, and knowing you, it will probably happen that way. We have known each other for a long time, Jacob, and I want you to know I have a lot of respect for you. You play the game fair and that's the way I like it. The time you spent with the marines in the South Pacific during the war help build your character. My brother was your commanding officer and he talked about you a lot."

"Thanks Lieutenant, you can always count on my cooperation. Should I find something of importance to attach to this slimy bastard, you'll be the first to know."

*　*　*

After the body was removed and the police had left, Jacob sat at his desk. The whole office was one room about 30 feet by 20 feet. He had a small private office space walled off with tinted glass. It did not reach the ceiling, which happened to be around 12 feet high in this old building. The window from his second floor office overlooked Hollywood Boulevard to the west. It was the only window in the office. The air conditioning was central and, at times, it didn't work properly, which made it stuffy for the reception area. There were only two chairs for clients to sit on, both in his office and the reception area.

He decided to call Helen Billings to hear her reaction on Louis' departure from planet Earth. After six rings, there was still no answer. He hung up, took a walk down the stairs and headed straight for the front door. There was still a commotion going on outside. The curious wanted to know from the police what was going on or what had happened. The officer, who obviously had a strong sense of humor and some dislike for him, was telling the curious ones that some crazy "gumshoe," and by that he meant Jacob, had killed himself. When the officer saw him coming out the door, Jacob thought he detected a bit of immediate redness on his face. He pretended he had not heard him and kept on walking towards Schwab's for coffee. Some of the studio crowds were regulars at the lunch counter.

*** 

As Jacob walked inside, he could see there were a few "wanna be's" sipping early morning coffee, probably spiced up. The gumshoe sat at the counter and was served a hot mug of his favorite Java.

Jennie, the waitress, blurted out; "What's going on in your building, flatfoot? I hear some guy got bumped off right in front of your desk. Is that true?"

She stood there looking straight at him waiting for an answer. Her question had not disturbed anyone else in the joint. This is Hollywood you know. The patrons were used to hearing actors reciting script lines aloud, so this one was no different to them. To Jacob it was. "Yes, Jennie," he said, "some poor bastard was sent to the Promised Land without a return ticket. He didn't even have a chance to speak to me about it. How do you like that? I'm glad I wasn't in the office when it happened. You know, I could be following his deadly footsteps," the proud PI said with a smile.

She smiled showing those big white molars and walked away without saying a word. Death had become a mystified event in the world of dreamers aspiring to become part of the big screen. Someone being shot and killed in an office, to them, was no different from someone being shot "à la Al Capone" on the big screen in a movie theater. The private eye gulped his coffee and ordered a fresh one to go. He took a walk back to reality, his second floor office.

\*\*\*

When he arrived at the building, all bystanders were gone. Even the police officer that had been standing guard had left. He walked up the stairs as fast as he could. Somehow Jacob had the feeling the police had overlooked something. What that something was, he couldn't tell right away but would give it a shot. To his surprise, Anne had already arrived. "You're early Miss Dombrowski," he said in an official tone. "Did you hear about the guy being snuffed out right here in the office?"

"First of all, Jacob, it's after ten. Secondly, the police officer that was standing guard outside the main entrance joyfully filled me in on the morning news. Now if you would like to supply me with more details, I'm willing to listen. Was this guy a client of ours? On the other hand, is it a case of wrong identity? Don't look surprised, Jacob, you know what I mean. Was it supposed to be you?"

"You know, Anne, you would have made a good prosecutor. Maybe you should go back to UCLA and pursue a law degree. Questions, questions, you fire them like a machine gun. This is what makes you so efficient in this business. No, the guy was not a client, but the husband of a client. You remember Helen Billings; she hired me to find dirt on her husband. She was going to file for divorce and just needed additional bits and pieces to blow him away. I did find some items of interest on Louis-the-snake Billings. I know the case was due for court shortly, but now, she won't have to go through the mudslinging. I wonder if she had him removed from the society registry. Do you think Helen Billings could have done it?" Jacob said. "There were no signs of struggle, which usually is a telling tale the victim knew the assailant."

Anne answered, "From what I can recall of the little lady, I don't think Helen Billings is capable of committing premeditated murder. Hiring someone to do it, that's another story. I remember how small she is physically from her first visit here. Barely over five feet tall and maybe 100 lbs., kind of a shy person, not your normal description of a hit-man. No, I don't think she could have done it Jacob. Here's the file on Mrs. Billings, including the photos you took of her husband with what appears to be call- girls. Have you talked to her about it yet?"

"No, Anne, I tried once and no one answered the telephone. It just kept on ringing. After six or seven rings, I hung up." As he opened the file, Jacob noticed the telephone number listed didn't look like the number he had called earlier. Jacob walked to his desk and came back with Helen Billings' card. "Guess what? The last two digits are 98 and old dummy here dialed 89 as written on my card. I must have transposed the numbers in that manner when I took them from your file. I had better give her a call again. Thanks for enlightening me, as usual."